MAYHEM ON THE MARGATE

Rumbles on the Rails Book One

MICHAEL CLUTTERBUCK

HEDDON PUBLISHING

First edition published in 2023 by Heddon Publishing.

Print ISBN 978-1-913166-80-9
Ebook ISBN 978-1-913166-81-6

Cover design by Catherine Clarke Design
www.catherineclarkedesign.co.uk

www.heddonpublishing.com
www.facebook.com/heddonpublishing
@PublishHeddon

Michael Clutterbuck is a retired schoolteacher living in Melbourne, Australia with his wife, two children and five grandchildren. He was born in 1937, brought up in Chester in a railway family, and was educated at the King's School and Manchester University. After his training as a language teacher, he spent four years in Hamburg, where he married. He and his wife migrated to Australia in 1965. He spent twenty-five years teaching at a school in Melbourne, followed by another twelve years teaching academic English to young Asian adults at Monash University, finally retiring in 2004. He co-authored a set of English exam preparation tests before writing the *Steaming Into* series of seven books of railway fiction published by Heddon in the UK. *Mayhem on the Margate* is the first book in a new series of railway crime stories.

Praise for the Steaming Into series

"One of the best books of its kind. Hats off to the author. So good I have bought all the other books in the same series."

"Right from the start you could smell the smoke and hear the clank of metal wheels on iron rails. Back to a time of the dark days of war. The men who worked so hard to keep the country moving the story runs from the beginning of the war though to the end. A story that in parts is funny and in others so sad, I found this a good read for the start of what life was like for the men who ran it, a time now long gone but still remembered."

"Being a steam enthusiast I am probably biased, but this book is an extremely good history of what it was like to be operating steam trains during the bombing. This author has apparently written more books on the subject which I intend to read. Very absorbing."

"When I first read this, I couldn't believe it was a work of fiction. The author has done his research into the intricacies and politics of men working on the steam locomotive footplate. The attention to detail is brilliant the background stories are also very interesting. Highly recommended to those who have an interest in Steam Locomotives and the crews that worked on them."

This is for Christa

INTRODUCTION

After writing 140 short railway stories in the seven books of the *Steaming Into* series, featuring the enginemen in steam trains, I decided to try a different type of story, based on the concept of poetic justice, and with no reference to railways at all. This has proved to be rather more difficult than I had assumed, as the following tale will show.

Some writers are, I understand, inclined to rough out their plots in their heads, often before they even sit down to type out the first draft. I have never done this. Indeed, if I have the germ of an incident, I sit down at my ancient Apple Mac and begin to type, without the slightest notion of how (or even whether) a story will unfold. Over the following weeks, the same thing happens every time I sit down to compose. It is as if the computer plans a continuation and waits for me to attend to it once more, in order for it to guide me into writing what it has prepared. I expect any psychologist would tell me not to imagine such nonsense, and that in between writing bouts my brain has been subconsciously planning how the plot will develop. Well, be that as it may, I note that in this particular story, not only has a railway background eased itself into the tale, but two of the earlier featured enginemen from the *Steaming Into* books, Driver Denton and Fireman Hargreaves, have somehow managed to insinuate themselves as well.

Michael Clutterbuck, Melbourne. 2023.

Map of the Margate route

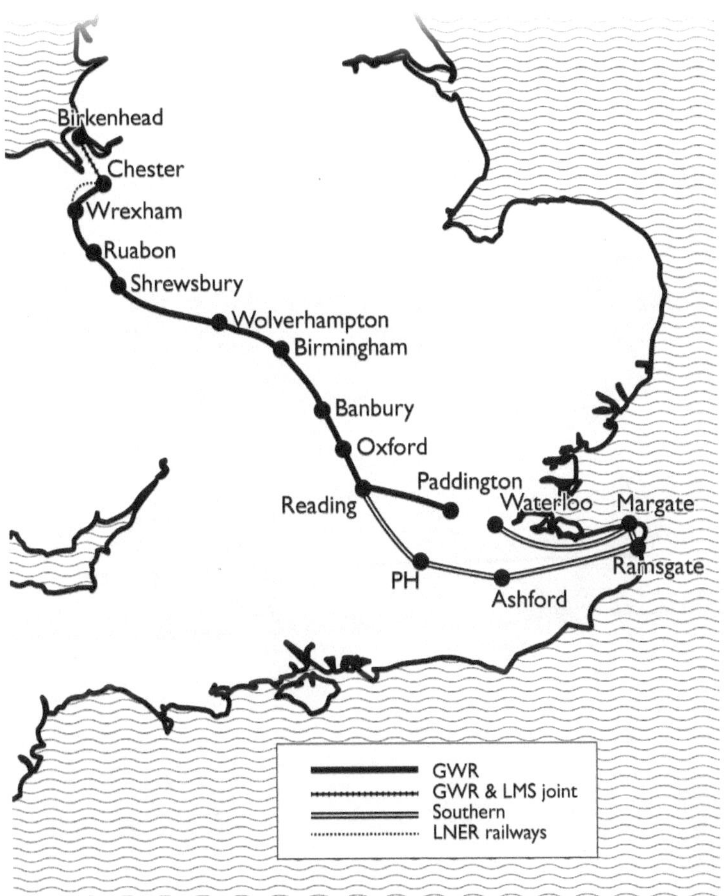

CHAPTER 1

The Offence

A small group of young children in Birkenhead were building with the broken bricks they had dug out from an area around the shattered houses. They knew they were not supposed to be there; their parents had warned them often enough about playing in the suburban bombsites that peppered the streets, but they also knew that after an air raid you could find all sorts of fascinating things where people's houses had once been. The hole in the fence had been too tempting to resist. It was seven-year-old Johnnie Kirkpatrick who noticed the round curve of metal stuck deep in the rubble where number 35 had been. He tried to dig it out with his hands but failed. He called for support.

"Hey, look what I found!"

The others crowded around to see.

"It's a part of bomb!" gulped one of the older lads. "Quick, get away from it!"

They all scurried off, but Johnnie slowed and turned to look again at his find. He picked up a half-brick and threw it at the piece of metal; it missed.

Some of the other children began to pick up stones or broken bricks, and started to throw them as well. This went on for two or three minutes until one of the missiles, larger than most, landed directly on the bomb. There was a huge blast and debris showered over the children as they hared away from the explosion.

When the smoke had cleared, shocked passers-by hurried through the torn fence to investigate. They saw five crying children, some with bleeding arms or faces. Two others were lying on the ground, not moving; one had lost a foot. Ambulances arrived swiftly and took all the children to hospital, where one child was pronounced dead on arrival. Johnnie, the boy who was missing a foot, was taken straight into emergency treatment. The doctor stabilised the child but instructed the senior nurse to ring Chester, saying he had no time to complete surgery; there were still more urgent cases from the arrival of a destroyer which had put down a U-boat but had casualties on board, some of them German.

Nurses treated the rest of the crying children, but none were thought to be seriously hurt; their tears came mainly from fright, and the fear of their parents discovering they had disobeyed instructions. They were patched up and their shocked parents were summoned to come and collect them.

The ambulance, with its young patient, and its bell ringing urgently, raced down the A41 into Chester, and drew up outside the Royal Infirmary, where hospital porters were waiting to transport the boy into surgery.

"Thanks for helping us out," said the nurse with the ambulance. "We're still busy with the wounded from that destroyer last week."

"Glad we can help with this lad," replied one of the porters as he took hold of the gurney and began to wheel it through the emergency entrance.

Mr Harry Mortimer, the chief surgeon, stood back and surveyed his patient carefully for several minutes, fear crowding his features. He was a dapper man in his late fifties, and a very experienced surgeon. He didn't at all like what he could see.

He turned to the senior nurse, shaking his head. "It's not working, Matron!"

Another, younger, nurse noticed a solitary tear running down the surgeon's cheek.

"I have done all I can, but I cannot help this child; this new drug is not doing its job as it should!" said the surgeon. "Where did we get it from?"

"I believe it came from —"

The matron stopped, as the anaesthetist interrupted urgently, "He's going, Mr Mortimer, and I can't do anything to stop him!"

"And there's nothing I can do either!" The surgeon spoke in despair, as the vital signs showed that young Johnnie Kirkpatrick was slipping away. All the theatre staff looked on in helpless sorrow as the boy died.

Mr Mortimer had watched in frustration as many

elderly patients had died under surgery over his long career, when the medication had failed in its efficacy. But he found it especially agonising when the patients were young children, at the start of their lives.

"I don't understand it. I should have been able to save that child!" he groaned, as nurses covered the body and prepared it for the post-mortem. "A lost foot should not have been fatal; that drug should have prevented this!" He looked at the matron. "Where did you say that medication came from?"

"It's from the batch we received last week, sir. The supplier told us we were lucky to get it; Birkenhead missed out, because there wasn't enough to go around. We won't get any more until next month."

"Do we have any left?"

"Yes, there are a few more phials."

"I want them analysed," said the surgeon grimly. "And I want to know where they came from."

Mortimer decided that he would contact a senior acquaintance in the city police; buying a pound of black-market ham was one thing – most were guilty of that from time to time – but supplying dodgy black-market medication was entirely another. This was surely murder.

"I'll send them for analysis immediately," said the nurse.

"And Matron, make certain that nobody else uses them until they have been found to be safe."

"Very good, Mr Mortimer."

The Royal Infirmary was the main hospital in the city, and could call on a team of several surgeons. Two days after the distressing incident with Johnnie, Harry Mortimer was in the doctors' lounge when the door opened and Jeremy Short, the hospital's pharmacist, came in. His expression was grave.

"I've got the initial analysis you asked for, Mr Mortimer. That whole batch of the drug is lethal; it looks as if it has been modified. It's had something added to it, to bulk it up. I don't yet know what that something is; that will take us a day or two more to check, but I thought you'd need to know straightaway."

"Thank you for the warning, Jeremy. You know I could have saved that child, if I'd had the genuine stuff. We'd better get the police in to check the origin of that batch. I've not heard of dubious medication being supplied on the black market, so we've never been much affected so far."

***

In a quiet suburb of Chester, fifteen miles from Birkenhead, Benjamin Charlton – a man whose appearance suggested he was surprisingly well-fed (an unusual circumstance in January 1945) – returned from a short visit to a contact in the American Army Air Force base at Padgate near Warrington, carrying a large box. Once safely in his house, he opened the box carefully and removed five of a number of small packages, before taking the box down to his cellar and carefully hiding it behind a false wall. Charlton made a brief phone call and half an hour later another, younger, man appeared.

Walter Smith was conservatively dressed in a smart suit, his black hair carefully combed, and his short moustache equally carefully trimmed. He didn't seem to be in any way incapacitated. Looking at him with some distaste, Charlton wondered again what the man had done to avoid being conscripted into the Forces.

Still, offensive though he might be, Smith was a useful man to know if you wanted anything hard to get, such as the gun he had obtained for Charlton some months back. Smith deposited a package onto the kitchen table and five large, black-and-white banknotes changed hands. He made to leave.

"The local paper reports a child died from substandard medication in hospital last week," remarked Charlton.

"Not your kid, was it?" Smith's cold eyes targeted him.

"Er – no, no."

"So what's the problem?"

Charlton changed the subject quickly. He pointed to the package on the table. "From Harrison or from Jonesy?" began Charlton, then stopped. "No," he said quickly. "I don't want to know, of course."

"Bloody stupid question," replied the young man, and he left.

One day, I'm going to have that insolent young puppy dealt with, Charlton thought grimly. He wasn't a violent man himself, but he had no hesitation in paying others to administer what he thought of as retribution for insulting behaviour. He laid out the five packages and proceeded to add a measured amount of powder from Smith's parcel to each.

***

Detective Inspector Roger Wolseley of the Chester City Police was unusual, in that he was still working at close to seventy years old, although he didn't look his age. He had planned to retire five years earlier, but had been persuaded to stay in the job for the duration of the war. Wolseley put down the paper he had been reading, muttering, "Six or so months and they'll have sorted the Germans out, and I can retire gracefully."

His phone rang. It was Detective Superintendent Henderson, and he sounded worried. "Vital job for you, Roger; another duff batch of a drug has been found at the Royal Infirmary. This time it's nasty stuff. See if you can trace its origin, will you? It was responsible for the death of a child there last week."

"Yessir, I'll get onto it right away."

Wolseley liked Henderson, who generally assumed his detectives were competent, and allowed them to get on with their jobs without interference.

"It's been going on too long, so keep me informed."

"I will, sir, but I have to say I've been after these people for months, and have got almost nowhere so far. But I'll keep at it."

Wolseley placed the handset back on its cradle thoughtfully. *If I get the bastard who supplied that, I'll make certain he's going down for murder.* He had no illusions about criminals during the war. The papers and magazines had extolled the increased social cohesion that was one of the few benefits of the last few years, but Roger knew from experience that the criminal element in society thrived. They relished the opportunities the blackout provided, and thefts and muggings were rife. The only advantage that he could see was that minor criminals could be persuaded to join the armed services, instead of languishing in prison. They could actually serve the society they had previously been robbing.

By May, DI Wolseley had still made very little progress, although he believed he had the germ of a lead. He was certain that three more similar deaths in Liverpool hospitals could be ascribed to the unwitting use of adulterated drugs, which made him more determined to find the supplier. However, national affairs overtook him. The war in Europe ended, and he immediately (and thankfully) retired from the force, leaving the black-market investigation to his successor, Inspector Daniel Williams, who believed that everything had to be done strictly by the book. Wolseley was sure that Williams would, quite frankly, make a dog's breakfast of the investigation.

In his own enquiries, Roger Wolseley had come across further information, but had neglected to report a possible lead. This case had become personal, and he did not trust Williams to deal with the investigation thoroughly. Now in retirement, he had the determination, the skills, and the time, to trace the perpetrator himself. Furthermore, he had always been of a thrifty nature, and had been careful to save up for his retirement, so shortage of funds was not a serious problem.

Throughout the country, wartime black-marketeers were being caught and dealt with by the courts, but Wolseley's personal quarry proved extremely elusive, until a lucky break in October 1945. Newspapers had reported the arrest of an American officer at the airbase at Padgate, who had been stealing medication and selling it on the black market. Wolseley knew one of the US Army Air Force police officers there; the two had co-operated on an earlier crime, and he had noticed a detail on the American's papers which the USAAF police had not chased up. There had been a suggestion that an English criminal was involved, but no trace of him was found.

It was Wolseley's opinion that his successor had been lazy in the investigation. He began a long and thorough search, which took him to an address in the Vicar's Cross area of Chester. A quiet word from an ex-colleague gave him the name of the owner of the house, and two months' careful observation of the owner's activities provided further clues, until he knew he had his man.

***

One morning in early January, Ben Charlton heard the early post arrive. He collected two letters from the letterbox in his front door. One he recognised from his bank. He smiled with pleasure; this would inform him how much more the recent package deal had deposited into his already very gratifying account. The war had been a nuisance, of course, but if you knew the right people, it could be very profitable. The second letter was addressed in a hand he did not recognise. He opened it and began to read.

His heart skipped a beat.

The letter threatened serious reprisals for the harm done from the medication Charlton had supplied. But Charlton had only used the medication he bought from that Yank, and the stuff from Smith to mix in with it, so any damage would have to be Smith's problem, not his. Even so, the writer seemed to know a great deal more about his affairs than anyone ought to. But who had the letter come from, and what did they want from him? If it was the police, they would have been round already, and in any case, he had paid that senior copper well enough to keep him informed of matters which might concern him. It had to be someone else, with a personal motive; perhaps some criminal's relative had been on the receiving end of the faulty drug? He had better make himself scarce, and quickly, but where could he go?

Gulping his breakfast down, Charlton had a flash of inspiration. Margate. It was at the other end of the country; he was bound to be safe! He had met a smuggler at a hotel there two years previously and had made a note of the place, in case he ever needed to get away quickly.

Charlton rang the station and was told that a train to Margate would be leaving early next morning. Perfect. He could spend the day getting his belongings together and be on the South Coast by the following afternoon.

At a quarter to eight the following morning, Charlton climbed out of the taxi, paid the driver, and hurried into the entrance of Chester General Station, struggling with his heavy suitcase and gazing worriedly around him. He knew that his stature might draw attention; an obviously well-fed man was a rare sight in post-war Britain, where excess weight suggested either a very senior and responsible position, or serious business acumen (this latter implying the possibility of a disregard for the laws of the realm). Cursing his greedy nature, he wished that he could blend in with the crowd.

He lowered his case to the ground to catch his breath as he purchased his return ticket to the South Coast. His gaze swept around the space in front of the booking office, but he was relieved to note that none of the other passengers seemed to be paying attention to him. He in turn paid no attention to the elderly man behind him in the queue.

Slipping his change into his pocket, Charlton picked up his case and headed off to show his ticket to the inspector at the gate.

"Margate, sir? Platform Two; due to leave in about twenty minutes. Just check with the guard on the train that you have the right coach, sir; some of the coaches are for other South Coast destinations."

Charlton nodded his thanks and turned left to walk along to the platform. There were already many people waiting and he inserted himself into the crowd, standing next to his suitcase and glancing nervously around from time to time.

***

Roger Wolseley had always looked after himself, and kept as fit as his career had allowed. He had never married, mainly because he had never found a woman with whom he wanted to share his life. He had certainly enjoyed a few casual attachments – he had a certain charm which seemed attractive to women – but they had never led to anything more permanent. He had always been of a solitary disposition, and his favourite hobby was walking in the fells of the Lake District, or across the Pennines. He was a competent cook, who enjoyed experimenting with exotic foods, although this particular interest had of course been severely curtailed during the war. Wolseley planned to develop his stamp collection in his retirement, but for the time being this project was put on hold while he concentrated his efforts on nailing the bastard who had been responsible for the deaths of at least one child, and four other hospital patients, all for the sake of a generous bank balance and comfortable lifestyle.

He sidled into the crowd, to a position from which he could observe his quarry without attracting the man's attention. Wolseley carried an ex-military haversack over his shoulder, with a spare set of clothing and one or two other items that might prove helpful if an opportunity arose. He had been careful to pack his pills; he had found over the years that in times of serious stress (and there had been plenty of those) the occasional strong relaxant had helped him sleep. Wolseley doubted very much that his target would register him; he knew his appearance was fairly benign. An older gentleman, of medium height, and no real distinguishing features; his hair was nondescript brown, albeit now tinged with a few grey streaks, and his jacket and trousers were well worn. His overcoat looked exactly as one would expect it to look after twenty years of constant wear. In fact, he knew he would not stand out in any crowd; an advantage that Roger had often found helpful in his career.

The ex-DI knew perfectly well that what he was planning would be illegal, and possibly even criminal, and potentially he risked a lengthy prison sentence. Yet equally, he was not convinced that the law would be certain to administer the death penalty to a black-marketeer who sold lethal medication. This man had proved himself to be both clever and elusive, and might be able to argue his way to a lesser penalty. This potential wrong was going to be righted, determined Wolseley (wondering briefly whether 'righted' was a verb; he liked his grammar to be correct). What precisely he was going to do, Wolseley had not quite decided, but it should lead to a fatality. That much was definite.

CHAPTER 2

Opening Gambit

It was a cold early January morning as Driver George Denton strode towards the locomotive office. Here, drivers would find out what their duties were for the day, and who their fireman would be. Railway companies had long discovered that it was best if good teams were kept together as far as possible, because their trains were more likely to be run efficiently, but of course there were occasions when this was not the case – perhaps on account of illness, or holidays due – and pairs needed to be rearranged. Discovering the name of a replacement would usually be followed by an expression of surprise, pleasure, or sometimes disappointment.

George saw that he and his regular fireman, young Lance Hargreaves, were to take the 8.18 morning express as far as Wolverhampton that morning; the train itself was the daily express from Birkenhead to the South Coast, but Chester crewmen changed at Wolverhampton and handed over to an Oxford or Wolverhampton crew, before returning to Chester on the 12.12 from Paddington. All in all, this constituted a day's duty. George and Lance knew this it well, having done it for several years. It wasn't unduly challenging, although that could depend on the type and condition of the locomotives. The usual locomotive for this run was an express passenger Castle class engine, fast and strong as they were, but if an engine was overdue for servicing, that was a very different matter. The hilly stretches between Shrewsbury and Chester could easily test the experience of any crew, but George Denton had a reputation in Chester Shed as one of its best drivers, and he had no fears of running out of steam, especially when he had Lance Hargreaves as his mate. Lance was the most competent young fireman he had ever worked with, and they formed a team which had already established a reputation in the whole division, from Birkenhead to Banbury. Lance was short and stocky, but powerfully built. He had left school early but was by no means unintelligent, and he had a fast and ready wit; although, it had to be said, his language left a great deal to be desired.

As he left the enginemen's cabin to head for their locomotive, George thought he recognised the familiar figure of his fireman walking towards him through the early morning gloom. They were to take a new County class 4-6-0 locomotive on the express to the South, known to railwaymen in Chester as 'the Margate'. The Counties were brand-new engines and had a dubious reputation among crews; they had been built and hurried into service at the end of the war, and had not had the usual thorough testing that the GWR normally put their new engines through. Consequently, many enginemen did not know how to get the best out of them, complaining that they ran out of steam on the hills. George liked the Counties, though, and felt that if they were carefully handled they could outmatch even the Castles on the hilly sections.

There were several daily Great Western expresses from Birkenhead to the South, but most of them terminated at Paddington – although, destined for the South Coast, this particular one did not. The GWR expresses to the South originated as a rival service to the LMS between Euston and Liverpool, although most informed travellers between London and Merseyside used the LMS route, which got its passengers to Liverpool almost two hours faster, claiming the GWR deserved its nickname of the 'Great Way Round'. The problem for the GWR was that the run from Paddington necessitated two changes of locomotive – one at Wolverhampton, and the second at Chester, where the route reversed – and then finally the crossing the Mersey by way of the ferry from Woodside Station, or the Mersey Railway from Rock Ferry, under the river.

Lance had a grin on his face as he greeted his driver. "I could a' done wiv a sleep-in today, Mr D."

"Oh yes? Out with a young lady last night, were you, Lance?" George Denton was under no illusions about the lad's interest in the opposite sex. He had once commented to the shedmaster, Sidney Thomson, that the 'L' in Lance's name ought to stand for 'Lechery' but that, in spite of the boy's sexual shenanigans, he had the makings of a cracking fireman, and even driver.

"Yes, George, I'm inclined to agree with you," Sid had replied, "but he's a cheeky little sod, and I've had to bounce him more than once."

"Now then, Mr D, what've we got on the Margate this mornin'?" asked Lance, as he joined his driver to find their locomotive.

"We've got that County we had last week, Lance. We're going to have to get used to it. Personally, I like the Counties, but they have to be handled differently from the usual Castles and Stars, and some of the lads don't like them."

"So I'm goin' to be learnin' agen?"

"Indeed you are."

***

Among the passengers at Chester General Station, two children waited with their father on Platform Two, for the incoming South Coast Express from Birkenhead, which they would take as far as Oxford. There they would meet their aunt, who would come to the station to chat to them while they waited twenty minutes for the Paddington connection; she might even bring them biscuits, and tea in a Thermos. William Hoyle, their father, was taking them to London to see a pantomime; they would arrive in the early afternoon, and would go to a Lyons Corner House for tea, see the show, and stay a night in a hotel, returning home the next day from Paddington. It was going to be a long and exciting two days; they would be very tired, but it would be worth it. They could tell their friends all about their excitement when the spring term began at school the following week.

At eight years old, Jimmy Hoyle was looking with envy at older boys with long trousers, wishing he were old enough to be able to protect his legs from the cold wind like they could. His sister, six-year-old May, didn't seem to care about the wind, but then she was wearing woollen leggings under her skirt, so probably didn't feel it like he did. However, Jimmy's worries about the wind were swept aside as he heard the whistle of an approaching train. He turned to see the front of the locomotive approaching their platform, and turned to his sister.

"Our train," he announced with superior authority. He knew it was their train to London because, as it curved into the platform, he could see that the coaches had big windows and corridors. Most of the Chester-Birkenhead trains were locals with non-corridor coaches; they only had smaller windows, and doors to every compartment. He didn't like these because every time the train stopped, you had to put up with passengers opening your door and brushing your legs as they boarded or left. In the express, if you had a seat next to a large window, you were not at a doorway, and could watch what was going on outside without disturbance.

The approaching locomotive was a large Prairie 2-6-2T tank engine, which was the norm on this train, bringing the half-dozen coaches from Birkenhead into Number Two Bay. Here, the engine would be detached, and the train would reverse. The waiting express passenger County class locomotive, with its three or four strengthening coaches, would back onto the rear and then head back out with the ten or so carriages, heading towards the South.

Jimmy had noticed their father checking his watch and nodding in approval as their train came in. He knew why: their father was a timetable clerk, and was responsible for arranging the times of passenger trains through this whole area of the Great Western Railway, although exactly what this entailed, Jimmy wasn't sure; it just meant that Dad was an important man on the GWR. The children had witnessed this as they entered the station: their father had chatted to the ticket inspector at the gate, who had immediately let them through with a smile *without even checking their tickets!* Not only that but, although the last coach on their train was locked, to Jimmy's surprise his dad had taken a curious-looking key from his pocket and unlocked the door with it. They had climbed in and walked along the corridor.

May called excitedly, "Here, Daddy, this first compartment is empty!"

"No, May, not that one. Let's go to the middle of the coach," said Jimmy, once more showing his superior knowledge. "It'll be smoother."

Their father smiled at the comment. "Why, Jimmy? Why will it be smoother?"

"At the two ends of the coach, Dad, you'll be over

one of the bogies, but in the centre, you'll be between them, and it won't be so bumpy."

"Well done. We'll make a railwayman of you yet."

May sat down and settled her doll next to her. "Now you be good, Shirley, and sit nicely."

Jimmy headed straight to the window seat so he could stare out. Their father put his case on the luggage rack, took out the day's newspaper, and sat down to read.

"You're facing the wrong way, Jimmy," said May, pointing behind him in triumph. "The train's going this way."

Jimmy was going to enjoy himself: he pointed across to where the large locomotive with four green Southern Railway coaches was slowly moving out. The new County class locomotive was gleaming clean and shiny; a most unusual sight in these days of grimy engines, which in most cases hadn't been cleaned for years.

"That's our engine, May."

"It's already leaving, silly; it can't be our train." It wasn't often that May got the better of her brother, and she relished the moment. But her pleasure was short-lived, as they felt a gentle jerk soon afterwards. "What was that, Daddy?"

"They're giving us more coaches and a bigger engine, May."

Moments later, they felt the train gently begin to move, but May was going backwards, she noticed with disappointment. What was going on? She glimpsed Jimmy staring at her with a grin on his face.

He knew that was going to happen! She pointedly ignored him and addressed her doll. "Now, Shirley, have you got your sandwiches packed like I told you? We're going to be on this train for a long time, so you can take your coat off." She removed the doll's coat, folded it up, and placed it on the seat.

Jimmy shook his head. How was it that girls were always able to cheat their way out of being wrong? It wasn't fair!

As the train slowly made its way out of the platform, his injured feelings quickly gave way to deep interest as he slipped into the corridor to observe which engines he could see in the Great Western locomotive shed.

"There's three namers, Dad," he called to his father. "A Castle, a Hall, an' a Saint." A moment or two later, he announced excitedly, "An' there's an LMS Duchess on the turntable! Wait till I tell the boys in my class on Monday; they'll be green with envy!"

His dad looked up briefly and went back to his paper. Engines with names on them were always more interesting to most young boys, but his father knew that freight engines often brought bigger profits to the four big companies.

As Jimmy was studying the engines on shed, a portly man walked past their compartment with what appeared to be a heavy suitcase, judging by his grimace. The man stopped, slid the door open and, grunting, lifted his case, clearly labelled 'B. Charlton', onto the rack.

He lowered his large posterior onto the seat

opposite Jimmy's with relief, much to the boy's annoyance. Jimmy had hoped the seat would remain vacant for much longer. He assumed the big man would settle and read a newspaper as his dad was doing, but the man just kept on looking through the wide window, and then peering out to the corridor. He just couldn't seem to keep still, as if he were a bit frightened. But why should such a large man be frightened? Jimmy looked at his father, but he had his face in his paper, and didn't seem to have noticed their fellow passenger.

Two ladies passed by in the corridor, and the man stared intently at them. What was wrong with him?

As the train entered the first of the two big tunnels outside the station and the compartment lights dimmed, Jimmy thought he saw a passing shadow in the corridor. The big man stood up and worked his way past Jimmy and his father to open the door and look out. Apparently seeing nothing to upset him, he returned to sit down again.

Why can't he just settle down? thought Jimmy. *He's just a bloody nuisance.* Suddenly both astounded and horrified at what he had almost said aloud, Jimmy felt his face turn very red. He had heard a man say those words to another man a few weeks back, and he knew that swearing was something that even parents occasionally did, but they were really angry if their children did so. Dad very rarely got angry, and he never had in public, but you couldn't be sure. Jimmy pressed his hand to his mouth, as if to keep his thoughts from turning into spoken words.

When the train was five minutes off its first stop, in Wrexham, a young man walked along the corridor, stopped, and stared into their compartment. The big man seemed to actually shake in fear, and looked carefully away until the young man passed. Jimmy watched surreptitiously as the man waited for two minutes before standing up, taking his case from the rack, and leaving the compartment. *Thank goodness for that.* Jimmy could now relax, and concentrate on enjoying the scenery.

***

In the locomotive cab, Driver Denton was watching, pleased at the way his fireman had managed up Gresford Bank.

"You've done well there, Lance. These Counties can run out of steam quite quickly and they can lose time, if you're not careful."

"Then why put 'em on the bigger expresses? Seems a daft idea."

"They've much the same power as a Castle, so can handle the same heavy expresses, but on the downhill run they can pick up steam again more quickly. This means that they're good for the hilly runs like ours, and the Devon and Cornwall stretches."

"So why use 'em for the long straight runs, then? Don't make sense."

"I think it's because the company is not yet sure where they are most suited. They're still finding out."

Lance directed another shovelful of coal into the left corner of the firebox. "One day, Mr D, I'd like to drive a King. I've never seen one up 'ere." The thirty Kings were the pride of the GWR express passenger fleet.

George looked across the cab at Lance. "Why's that then, Lance?"

"Why's wot?"

"Why don't we see Kings in Chester?"

"I dunno. Oh yeah! We don't 'ave fifteen-coach expresses up 'ere."

"I knew you were smart!"

***

By this time, the train guard, checking the tickets of the passengers who had joined the train at Chester, had reached and tried a toilet door, but when it wouldn't open he tapped, saying, "Ticket, please!" The door opened very slightly and a hand holding a ticket appeared. The guard checked it, clipped it, and handed it back. "Thank you, sir or madam!" he replied, grinning. The door closed quickly again.

***

In their compartment, May said, "Daddy, I have to go to the toilet." She got up and left, but she was back in half a minute, and sat down. "Someone's in there."

Mr Hoyle took his daughter to find the lavatory in the next carriage along.

Jimmy enjoyed a few minutes' peace and quiet. When his sister and father returned, he too got up to go to the toilet, only to find it still locked. He hadn't seen anyone passing by so presumably it was the same person. What was taking them so long? Deciding he didn't really want to know, he returned to the compartment, saying, "Our toilet is still locked, Dad. I'll just go along to the next carriage too."

"Someone with a problem, perhaps," remarked their father.

He had no inkling of quite how true that was going to be.

CHAPTER 3

One-all at Wolverhampton

Charlton was beginning to feel alarmed; he had been waiting in fear for over ten minutes now. Several passengers had tried to use the toilet, and it was only a matter of time before the guard would come back to investigate what the problem was with whoever was in there. Charlton would have to think of some excuse. He hadn't, he admitted to himself, seen anyone remotely suspicious, apart from the young man who had stared at him in the compartment where that damn kid had watched him all the time. It had even crossed his mind that the boy was something to do with it, but he knew that was ridiculous. He was becoming paranoid.

As the train pulled up at Ruabon, Charlton cautiously opened the toilet door and peered out. He saw the young man at the other end of the corridor, but he was holding a small case and preparing to leave the train. Once he was on the platform, a pretty girl ran over and embraced him. The two strode off together, laughing. Charlton sighed in relief; he had jumped to the wrong conclusion there. In any case, he thought, it seemed highly unlikely that whoever wrote that letter would be clever enough to anticipate his speedy escape at Chester Station, and follow him on a train to the South Coast, a twelve-hour journey. He began to feel more at ease.

Charlton proceeded with his case to find another First Class compartment – not that one with the nosy kid. He stalked along the train, looking for a preferably empty compartment, but this train was heavily loaded, even in First Class, and he had to sit with three other passengers in a coach near the front of the train. The only advantage he could think of was that, were it to turn out he was in danger, any violent and unwelcome action against his person would be witnessed by the other passengers; this might dissuade any adversary from, well – whatever he planned to do.

Charlton racked his brains to try and think of whom he might have annoyed sufficiently to threaten him. There would be plenty of options, he knew; but which of them was in a position to take the kind of action threatened in that letter? It obviously wasn't the police; they would have acted openly, so who the hell was it? He couldn't imagine.

There was, of course, that American officer from whom he had bought some of his wares; the Yank had demanded a king's ransom for the drugs, but Charlton had refused to meet such an exorbitant demand. The officer had been raging, but the US Army Air Force police had caught him and sent him for a long stretch in a US prison, and there had been nobody else, so who the hell was after him?

Perhaps a break by the South Coast would give him the space he needed to work it out. Then, once he had established who was after him, he would be able to sort out the problem. He had always been able to call upon two or three men (he didn't think of them as thugs, although he knew that's what they were) who, for a small fee, could be relied upon to persuade others to understand the wisdom of complying with Ben Charlton's requests.

***

Two coaches to the rear, Wolseley was also sitting and thinking. What exactly was he going to do about Charlton? He knew where the man was, and he had disguised himself in case Charlton recognised him, although he very much doubted that he would. Wolseley had, admittedly, walked past the man's house twice, but had been careful never to loiter long enough to raise any suspicion. Consequently, he was fairly sure that Charlton was unaware of how close his nemesis was. From Charlton's point of view, he would be simply another elderly man on a train with many others. Nevertheless, care would be necessary, as Charlton had many times proved how cautious he was. Indeed, he had only yesterday morning received the letter, but had spent the rest of the day packing, and was already off on the early train this morning. Wolseley was very thankful he had sacrificed his evening at home to keep an eye on

Charlton's house. This rapid getaway smacked of panic, and was an excellent sign. Not only had he got the bastard on the run, he even knew his destination! Standing behind him at the ticket office queue, he had clearly heard his quarry's destination.

Fortunately, the train had a buffet car, and Wolseley was able to grab a cup of tea and a sandwich, but the need for a sleep was compelling. He settled himself back in his corner seat and, on the presumption that Charlton would stay on this train through to its terminus at Margate, he decided to risk a short sleep.

Like most experienced detectives on observation, Wolseley could time himself, and he woke up much refreshed as the train was departing from Shrewsbury. But when he strolled past Charlton's compartment, he was shocked to discover that the man and his suitcase were no longer there. The ex-DI doubled back, checking all the toilet doors, but apparently none were occupied, so he went further back along the train, peering into all the compartments. In the last-but-one coach, he spotted Charlton reading a book. Wolseley stopped, carefully peering out of the window, and did not pass the compartment, instead returning to his seat near the front of the train, so that Charlton would not get a good look at him.

As he was walking back, Wolseley met the ticket collector. "Excuse me, could you please tell me what the next few stops are?"

"Certainly, sir. Wellington in about ten minutes; then Wolverhampton, Birmingham, Leamington Spa, Banbury, and Oxford. We'll be in Oxford at 12.22. I go off-duty there, and a Southern man takes over."

Wolseley nodded. "Very helpful, thank you."

"You're welcome, sir."

With a mental sigh, Wolseley returned to his seat, thinking that he was going to be frequently on the move over the next couple of hours, and that was only as far as Oxford. The train was not due into Margate until a quarter to five! Perhaps he could manage some kind of action before then.

At Wellington, Wolseley moved into the corridor to check the platform; it was unlikely, but not impossible, that Charlton would jump out and slip away. But he stayed put, and a relieved Wolseley went back to his place.

***

In another compartment, Jimmy noticed with concern that their father had dozed off. He looked meaningfully at his sister and pointed to their father.

"What?" whispered May.

Jimmy mimed eating a sandwich and May frowned, then understood, and nodded.

"Daddy, is it lunchtime?" she asked loudly.

Their father woke up and looked out of the window. "Where are we?" he asked.

"We've just passed Cosford, Dad," said Jimmy, who had been keeping an eye on the passing stations.

"Yes, definitely time for lunch," said their father, getting up and taking a wrapped parcel down from the rack.

The children both smiled expectantly; they knew a special treat was coming, and their mouths watered. Today, they were getting sandwiches with a special sandwich spread which they both loved. It was expensive, and a rare treat. Normally, their sandwiches contained apricot jam, which Jimmy was beginning to dislike purely because it appeared so often on their plates. Dad had explained that it was cheaper than strawberry jam at the Co-op, where he normally did the shopping.

Being a railwayman, their father could take his children cheaply on the train with Privilege tickets, which entitled his dependants to travel for about a third of the normal fare. This meant that holidays in distant places could be expected once a year, and the children rejoiced in them. The sandwiches, all too quickly consumed, were succeeded by another treat: a cold bottle of lemonade. This was shared by the two children (each watching that the other did not swallow too much).

Leaning back with satisfaction, Jimmy returned his gaze to the window before an uncontrolled burp escaped him. In embarrassment, he muttered "Pardon!" to the compartment's other inhabitants, who politely ignored him.

***

In the cab of the engine, Fireman Hargreaves was clearing the floor of coal dust, in order to leave the cab clean before uncoupling it from the train at Wolverhampton and taking it into the shed for servicing. Another engine would couple up and take the train further to Oxford, where a Southern Railway engine would take over for the rest of the run. He and Driver Denton would have their break and then find out which locomotive they would be taking back to their home shed at Chester.

When the train stopped at Wolverhampton Low Level station, Lance climbed down to uncouple the locomotive from the coaches. In the cab, George was joined by Inspector Harry Lynton.

"Mornin', George," said the inspector. "Problem this morning: change of duty for you both. Your fireman knows the road to Oxford, I believe?"

George sighed and his face fell; he knew what was coming. "Yes, he does, Harry. Have you let Sid Thomson know we'll be taking the train on?"

"Yes, I've phoned him. As you've no doubt gathered, the replacement crew is off sick. Sorry about that. Of course, you'll both stay at the railwaymen's hostel in Oxford and return on the Margate tomorrow, and get a day's extra leave."

"Can't be helped. What are we getting?"

"Actually, you're in luck. You've got a Star straight from the works after a sole and heel." (A 'sole and heel' was the railway term for a maintenance check, and included any minor repairs found to be necessary.) The Stars were older express passenger engines and in spite of their age were generally well-liked by enginemen because, like their younger sisters, the Castles, they were fast and powerful. The fact that their engine had just had a minor repair was a bonus; this was going to be a pleasure to drive.

Even now, after the war had ended, it was still rare to be given an engine in good nick. The railway workshops were still busily catching up on urgent repairs from wartime service.

"Ah, we should be thankful for small mercies, then."

"I've already informed your fireman before he could uncouple, by the way," the inspector added.

Lance was pleased at the chance of firing a locomotive fresh from the works; that didn't happen too often these days.

"Jus' one problem at Oxford, Mr D."

"Oh? What's that, Lance?"

"I 'aven't got me pyjamas."

"The academics won't like that," remarked George.

"The academics'll 'ave to lump it," responded Lance, angling his shovel in the firebox, and using the reflection to see where more coal might be needed to even the fire.

***

Nearing the Wolverhampton stop, Jimmy went into the corridor to watch from the other side of the train. The area they had entered was known as the Black Country, and the appellation was well deserved, with the region's succession of factories, bombsites, ash pits and smoky air, and general atmosphere of gloom. But Jimmy wasn't bothered; there was plenty of railway interest here. He was standing at the window, looking at other tracks leaving and joining the main line, when Charlton came along the corridor.

The latter winced as he saw that wretched boy again, but then he realised that the child could actually be useful. "Have you been standing here long, sonny?"

"About ten minutes," replied Jimmy.

"Tell me, have you seen a man walking up and down the train looking into the compartments?"

"Yes, the guard has been doing that."

"No, no," said Charlton impatiently. "I mean another man, not a railwayman." *Why do kids take things so literally?*

"Only an old gentleman," said Jimmy, thinking quickly.

"Old gentleman? What did he look like?"

"He had a small beard, a grey jacket, and brown trousers."

"Did you see him earlier as well?"

Jimmy puckered his forehead for a moment and then said, "I think so; I think he has passed a couple of times."

Charlton nodded briefly and walked on, thinking hard; was this old bloke someone he should be worried about? It might be worth keeping an eye open for a grey jacket and brown trousers. But an old, bearded bloke? It didn't sound like a man who would send threatening letters. Yet just as the train drew to a standstill, a man matching the boy's description appeared at the end of the corridor. Charlton stared at him then hurried to his seat, thinking fast. He grabbed his case and walked quickly to the coach door, descending onto the platform.

***

Wolseley, surprised at seeing Charlton, watched the man leave the train. He hurried back to his own seat, grabbed his haversack, and also disembarked. The stop here was longer, because more coaches were being attached, and Wolseley looked amongst the many passengers but couldn't see Charlton, until the whistle sounded, and the guard waved his green flag. The train began to move off and, as it did so, Wolseley caught sight of Charlton among a small group of people on the platform. Then he saw him reach out for a door, open it, and jump back onto the moving train. Moving fast, Wolseley did the same, wondering whether his own move had been observed. He went back to the last coach to give himself time to think. Charlton would have certainly seen him leave the train but, with any luck, he would have been too busy sorting himself out to have seen him reboard.

***

Jimmy was having a fascinating time. Not only had he seen the new engine waiting to add its coaches to strengthen the train (he didn't say 'add to', because he knew railwaymen said 'strengthen'), but he had also observed that fat man leave in a hurry, and then the old gentleman do the same… and then he saw both of them jump back on. It was all very exciting. *Something to tell Dad and May!*

***

Unlike Jimmy, Charlton was not excited. He was worried. At the very least, he knew for certain now that he was being followed, and had a description of the man who was on his tail. The question was what to do about it.

He opened his case and lifted the shirts and ties to check that his gun was still securely in its place, as well as the top bundle of ten fifty-pound notes. He had hoped that he wouldn't need to use these, but he was glad he had packed them. There was another similar bundle of notes under his shirts and underwear, for emergencies. *A shame this isn't America*, he thought.

Here, it didn't pay to go round shooting people. The British police took a very dim view of crimes involving guns. If anyone died, you could easily find yourself standing with a bit of rope around your neck and wondering why you hadn't chosen a safer way of life. Charlton knew he was going to have to be very careful indeed if he didn't want his collar felt by some copper. He returned to his seat and, placing his suitcase back on the luggage rack, he sat down and opened a newspaper, to hide his face from the other passengers while he pondered his situation.

***

In the train's last coach, Wolseley was also considering his next move. It was clear that more guile was required. After the little mishap at Wolverhampton, Charlton knew he was being followed, and who his pursuer was. He would be on the lookout. *We shall have to see*, considered Wolseley, *what opportunities the next stop in Birmingham offers.*

So far, the game stood at one-all. The next stop was Birmingham's Snow Hill, which was a very large station, and many passengers would be milling about. Surely something could be organised to drive Charlton into desperation, during which he might make a foolish decision, providing Wolseley with a situation he could exploit?

Wolseley slipped into the toilet, took off his false beard, and turned his jacket inside-out. He was fond of this jacket, which had many times proved invaluable in his surveillance duties. He had bought it at a clothing store for stage costumes. He also replaced his trousers with the spare grey pair from his haversack. Charlton might still recognise him if he looked closely, but would hopefully miss him at a superficial glance. Wolseley looked at himself in the mirror, then practised his limp again. He hadn't used the limp for months, and wished he had a stick to go with it. He returned to his seat once more, and was ignored by the other passengers in the compartment. If they thought anything at all, they would just assume that the bearded man had left and another passenger taken his seat.

The train was now passing through the sidings of the approach to Snow Hill. *Time,* thought Wolseley, *to think of a new method to drive Charlton into some rash action.* What would make him angry enough to do something very ill-advised?

CHAPTER 4

Jimmy's dilemma

Snow Hill Station was by far the largest station on the Birkenhead-Paddington run, apart from Paddington itself, and it was always busy with passengers changing trains for many different destinations. On the North-South run, they could change for places such as Bristol and the West Country, for Cardiff and South Wales, as well as West Midlands destinations. Consequently, when a train from Birkenhead to the South Coast came in, there were always many people leaving and boarding, on the up main platform. This milling about would, Wolseley hoped, give him an opportunity to rattle Charlton's cage, and drive the villain into some incautious act. Now, what could he do to speed up the process?

He was pondering this when the train slowed to an eventual standstill. There was a wounded soldier on the platform, and this gave Wolseley an idea. He would play the part of an injured man and find a seat in the same compartment as Charlton. People tended to be kindly disposed towards the wounded. He knew his disguise would not survive close observation for long. In fact, he was hoping Charlton would soon recognise him, lose composure, and thus act unwisely. How Wolseley would utilise this, he did not yet know; it would depend on exactly what Charlton did. In his career, Wolseley had often found it necessary to react quickly to an unanticipated situation, and had rarely failed to respond with success.

He walked back to Charlton's compartment and, limping, took a seat, tossing his haversack onto the luggage rack then proceeding to rest while gazing earnestly at his prey. One passenger stared at him in ill-disguised surprise. What was an elderly man with only an ex-army haversack and badly-fitting clothing doing in First Class?

To begin with, Charlton ignored him but then, having glanced over two or three times, a puzzled frown slowly spread over his face. The other passengers looked up as, with a muffled oath, Charlton leapt out of his seat, left the compartment, and hurried along the corridor, out of the coach, and onto the platform.

Gotcha! thought Wolseley. *The man has panicked!*

"Oh dear!" he exclaimed to the other passengers, pointing to the rack. "The gentleman's forgotten his case! I'd better take it to him." He took the case and followed Charlton's exit from the compartment, but went instead to the toilet, entered, and locked the door. Using a handy little device he had confiscated from a burglar he once arrested, Wolseley opened

Charlton's case to examine the contents. He removed the gun, and a bundle of banknotes from on top of the shirts, before locking the case again. Before he did so, he noticed a scribbled note with the name of the Margate hotel Charlton had booked into.

"My, my, Benjamin," breathed Wolseley, pleased. "We *are* getting careless!" He came out of the toilet and glimpsed Charlton on the platform, adjusting his tie and hurrying back towards the train, so he waited in the corridor for him.

***

Sitting in the cab of the locomotive, while passengers were leaving and boarding the train, Driver George Denton was concerned. His fireman's face showed unusual discomfort and he was fidgeting, which was quite at odds with his normal placid demeanour. Lance was searching carefully along the platform.

"What's up, Lance?" George asked.

"Dunno exackly, Mr D, I think I've got the runs; there must be a bog on the platform somewhere. I 'ope I c'n find it quickly!" He left the cab to hurry off and relieve himself.

"That's all we need," muttered his driver. "Two years back near Frodsham, he peed in my tender. Now in Brum he's looking for a toilet! Why can't the young bugger learn to control his bodily functions?"

Strong language was extremely rare for George Denton but this, together with his memory of the Frodsham incident, offended his abstemious nature.

Then of course there was the question of time-keeping. They were allowed four minutes at Snow Hill, and Lance's bowels might demand further time, which could make them late into Oxford, unless they had a clear run. Unduly late arrivals had to be explained in a written report, which took time (and some ingenuity, if the details were embarrassing).

Charlton, hurrying in fear and glancing behind him, didn't see Lance coming out of the toilet. He ran straight into him, knocking his cap off.

"Hey! Look where yer goin', yer daft sod!" grunted Lance, picking his cap up. He was normally a patient man but was already feeling guilty at possibly making the train lose time, and hence was short-tempered.

Charlton gazed at the person he had run into, and saw a short young man who, judging by his clothing was obviously a lowly workman. He replied brusquely, "You need to mind your manners, fellow!"

Lance's blood boiled and he reached out for the big man's tie. Tightening his grip, he pulled Charlton towards his face, snarling, "Mind me manners? You're the bleeding idiot wot ran into me! I was jus' walkin' back ter me work!" He let go of the tie suddenly and Charlton overbalanced and almost fell. Lance ignored him, hurried back to the engine, and climbed into the cab.

"You alright now, Lance?" asked George.

"Yes, Mr D, but I'm glad we've got stops in Leamington and then Banbury before we get to Oxford. An' when we get there, I'll get summat from a chemist, wot'll clog me system."

"I'm glad to hear it," commented George drily, leaning out to look for the guard's green flag.

"An' a stupid passenger ran inter me; an' I 'ad ter – wot's the word…?" continued Lance as he studied the pressure and the water gauges.

"Remonstrate with him?"

"Yeah, I expec' that's it."

"You didn't hit him, did you?"

"No, Mr D. I bloody wanted to, but I 'ad ter get back 'ere, didn't I?"

"I admire your sense of duty, Lance. Now, there's your shovel, and there's plenty of coal in the tender, and a greedy firebox ready to receive it."

Lance peered into the firebox and paused, then went into the tender, picked up a small lump of coal, and examined it carefully. "The fire's right for a while Mr, D," he said. "I'll just need this nice round lump."

"What on earth for?" George stared at his fireman, and gradually a smile spread over his face. "Of course!" he chuckled. "I'd clean forgotten about that."

***

In the Hoyles' compartment, Jimmy was eagerly staring out of the window as the train was in an area he was unfamiliar with. He was wide-eyed with excitement, having seen a King class locomotive on the down main platform. It was presumably on a Birkenhead train, which would exchange the King at Wolverhampton for a Castle or a County for the further run to Chester.

"Did you see that King, Dad?"

"Yes, Jimmy, I did. But you won't see one at Oxford; it's not on a double red route." The GWR marked its routes with colours to indicate weight restrictions. Double red were the only routes the heavy Kings were permitted on.

"Is that why we don't get Kings in Chester?"

"Actually, no, it's not. Although Chester is the northern limit of the double red route, our ten- or eleven-coach trains don't warrant the use of a King. Castles, Halls and Counties can easily cope with them."

"Oh, so wha– Oh, look, Dad, there's that big man again. He's running along the platform!" Jimmy watched curiously as Charlton hurried past then paused and looked back, lifting his hands in surprise. "Now he's getting back into the train."

Mr Hoyle looked out of the window and commented, "I think he's forgotten his case and is going back for it." May took no interest – she had fallen asleep clutching her doll.

His dad's comment appeared to be accurate, because Jimmy saw the two men meet in the corridor, where the suitcase was exchanged. Charlton went back into his compartment and the elderly man watched him enter, waiting a moment or two before sliding his hand into his pocket, pulling out what looked remarkably like a gun, and checking it before tucking it away again quickly, as another person entered the corridor from the far end.

***

Wolseley had waited to see which coach Charlton would head for and had then placed himself by the door to give him the case, explaining, "I'm sorry, sir. I saw you leave the train without your case and, assuming you had forgotten it, took it to hand it to you on the platform."

Charlton was nonplussed. Paranoia was clearly getting the better of him; here was that chap who had come into his compartment, and he'd actually gone to the trouble of returning his case to him. It seemed an unlikely action for somebody out to get him.

In his relief, he remembered his manners. "That's really most kind of you; I had indeed forgotten it. Don't know how that could have occurred."

Wolseley nodded. "Yes, we all slip up occasionally," he murmured, as he watched Charlton head back into the compartment, then briefly pulled out the gun from his pocket, to check the safety catch. He didn't notice a shocked Jimmy observing the meeting.

***

Shortly after they left the tunnel south of Snow Hill, George looked at his fireman. "Ready, Lance?"

His fireman paused in his work and picked up his lump of coal. "Yeah!" He grinned. "It was round 'ere, wasn't it?"

A member of the public had put a potty on a stake in his back yard, which bordered the railway, and most passing firemen couldn't resist the temptation to shy a piece of coal at it.

Lance waited. Seeing his target, he let fly, and was rewarded by the sight of the potty smashed into smithereens by his projectile. The shards fell to join the numerous lumps of coal lying just past the stake; he looked gleefully at his driver. "'E'll 'ave ter buy a new potty agen, Mr D!"

"He's very fortunate that you're not on a daily shift on this run, Lance. And he's got a week's worth of coal for free!" George chuckled as he turned his gaze once more through the front spectacle plate of the cab, to watch the track ahead.

***

Charlton sat more comfortably now, and relaxed. He hadn't seen the old man with the beard for some time. There were only two other people in the compartment. In addition to the old fellow who had returned his case and was now sitting opposite him, next to him was a youngish man who Charlton was sure had enjoyed a profitable war; he had an air of self-confidence and satisfaction – bordering on smugness. Charlton would put any money on the man having avoided military service. His was the face of someone who had used his talents for the purpose of expanding his bank account, probably with some assistance from the black market; this was not a man returning from any involvement in savage fighting for his life.

As the train left the Birmingham surroundings and entered a tunnel, the lights dimmed. When they came out into the open again, the man opposite had left, presumably to go to the toilet, because his haversack was still on the rack. Charlton picked up his paper again and began to read. As he did so, he noted a shadow in the corridor and looked up. *Good God, it's that old bearded fellow, and he's watching me!* He must have boarded the train again! But the man had vanished before Charlton opened the compartment door and peered out.

Two minutes later, the other passenger returned from the toilet and sat down with a smile and a nod, saying, "Must have been something I ate for breakfast this morning. Seems to have settled now." He took a book from his haversack and began to read, leaving Charlton totally confused and suspicious. Was he, or was he not, the same man as the bearded fellow? If that beard was false, it would have been easy to pop into the toilet and put it back on, and then slip back again and remove it. But what about the change of clothes? Was he a quick-change artist as well? Charlton began to wonder whether he was becoming completely irrational.

***

Things in the Hoyle compartment were also rather disturbing, at least for young Jimmy. He couldn't put out of his mind what he had witnessed, although he was starting to think he might have imagined the gun. Surely that old man was not the type to have a weapon concealed on his person.

Nevertheless, the boy was frightened: this was a serious matter, and the police ought to be told that a man with a gun was on the train.

"Jimmy, keep an eye on May while I go to the toilet," said his father.

Jimmy glanced at his little sister, but she was fast asleep, and Dad had told him to keep an eye on her. Like all little girls, she was a nuisance, but he didn't want anyone shooting her; she was his sister, after all. He sat there miserably, wondering what he should do. Was that really a gun he had seen? Or was it just a toy, to frighten somebody? Should he tell any of the other passengers in the compartment? What if the man threw it away before he could be arrested? Would the police accuse him, Jimmy, of wasting their time? Why did the elderly man have a gun – was he going to attack the fat man? What if there was a fight on the train? What if he shot the fat bloke? What if his dad got in the way and was shot? These and similar questions ran round Jimmy's brain and terrified him.

He sat and fidgeted for a while, then got up and went into the corridor to see if his dad was coming back; he would know what to do. Jimmy walked along as far as the toilet, which had the 'engaged' sign on the door; but it might be someone else in there anyway. Where could his dad be, if he wasn't in the toilet? Suddenly, Jimmy recalled that he was supposed to be keeping an eye on his little sister and he hurried back to their compartment, where all seemed to be well. None of the other passengers appeared interested in the goings on, and May was still fast asleep, her doll cuddled in her arms.

Tears were beginning to form in Jimmy's eyes; all this was getting to be too much. The trip to London to see a pantomime was supposed to be thrilling and exciting, but it was turning into a bloody nightmare. (The naughty word which had slipped out in his mind didn't worry him as it would have done a couple of hours earlier.)

What on earth was an eight-year-old boy to do?

CHAPTER 5

Charlton is relieved

On arriving in Leamington Spa, Driver Denton was pleased to note that Lance was in no hurry to visit the toilet on the platform.

"No problem with your rear end, Lance?"

"No, Mr D. I c'n 'old out for another 'alf an hour."

George nodded thankfully. The thought of another episode (and one considerably more unpleasant than that previous incident in his tender several years ago) was a great relief. He was also pleased at the condition of their locomotive. This Star class engine was now nearly forty years old and was performing well: Wolverhampton Works had done a good job on her. Furthermore, they would shortly be relieved by a Southern crew in Oxford, and then they could relax in the enginemen's hostel until their return on the Margate the following day.

"Just think, Lance, how our duties have improved recently. We get a lie-in at the hostel because we're not due back on the Margate until 1.47, and what's more, we can even relish the odd bacon sandwich again."

"Aye, an' there's summat else an' all. No bugger's goin' ter bounce a doodlebug on our 'eads agen, like they did a couple o' years back!"

George and Lance had suffered a flying bomb attack, which had put both of them in hospital, and had almost cost Lance his career.

"Very true, Lance. It's much pleasanter not to be having bombs and bullets aimed at us! I think I rather prefer this life."

"Mind you, Mr D, I did enjoy one part of me 'ospital stay; some 'o them nurses was pretty – now, wot's the word?"

"Obliging?"

"Yeah, that's it; obligin'. They was quite 'appy ter—"

"Spare me the details, Lance. Get your mind back on your duties!"

"An' there's me enjoyin' me thoughts! Yer c'n be cruel sometimes, Mr D."

George Denton shook his head sadly. *The lad's always got to have the final word!*

***

In his compartment, Jimmy almost cried in relief as his father came back, and he hurriedly brushed the tears from his eyes.

Mr Hoyle looked at him. "What's up, Jimmy?'

"Can we go into the corridor for a minute, Dad? There's something I need to tell you."

His father nodded and they slipped into the corridor, where Jimmy explained his fears.

"Now this is important, Jimmy," said his father, "are you quite certain that it was a gun you saw?"

"I think so, Dad. It looked exactly like my toy pistol, only bigger."

"Hmm," said Mr Hoyle. "Go and sit down with May. I'll be back in a few minutes."

Jimmy went back to sit with his sleeping sister, much relieved that the matter was now out of his hands; Dad would sort it out, he knew. Mr Hoyle walked back to the end of the train, where the guard had his office in the brake van. The latter had just finished checking the tickets of the passengers who had entered the train at Leamington Spa, and was writing up his journal. He looked up in surprise as Mr Hoyle came in.

"Good morning, Mr Hoyle, what can I do for you?"

"Sorry to interrupt you in your work, Gordon, but we may have a problem passenger on the train. My son thinks he saw a man with a gun in his pocket, possibly threatening another passenger, about ten minutes ago." He described the two men and what Jimmy had seen.

Guard Gordon Hewson stood up quickly and put his guard's cap on. "We'd better have a word with these gentlemen, then. I think I can recall where that older man sits, but I noticed that the younger one seems to move about in the train from time to time. I have wondered why." Over his years of service, Gordon Hewson had become very used to noting where passengers sat, especially if they attracted his attention for any reason.

The two men walked along the corridor until they saw Charlton; the guard poked his head into the compartment and asked if he could spare them a minute or two. Charlton looked startled, but nodded and joined them.

"Could I check your ticket please, sir?" Guard Hewson had developed an air of authority, which, with his official uniform and ticket punch, convinced most passengers to comply without demur with any request he made. Charlton was no exception and showed his ticket, wondering what this unusual request signified.

"Margate, sir; yes. Now, have you been troubled by any other passenger on this train today?"

What the hell? Charlton almost gasped aloud. *How did he know that?* Then he realised who the second man was; the father of that nosy kid. He must have seen something and told the guard. *Why can't people mind their own bloody business?*

"Not really, although one old man seems to have been following me around, I thought."

"Could you describe this man, sir?"

Charlton described Wolseley as he had last seen him in Wolverhampton, with a beard, and wearing a grey jacket and brown trousers.

He didn't mention his suspicion that it was the same man in disguise who had come into his compartment later, or that on leaving the train briefly at Snow Hill, only to reboard, he found the man waiting for him, with his case.

The guard nodded. "Yes, I have seen him, but he

left the train at Wolverhampton. Well, thank you for your time, sir."

As they walked back to the guard's van, Mr Hoyle said, "Did you notice the elderly man sitting opposite, in the fat man's compartment?"

"Funny you should say that, Mr Hoyle. I did. There was something about him that caught my attention, but I couldn't think what it was."

"He fits the description that my Jimmy gave me, Gordon. He also fits the description of the elderly man described by our large friend, although the clothing doesn't match, nor the lack of beard."

"Of course! I also thought it rather odd that a man with only an old ex-army haversack should be sitting in a First Class compartment. Could he have had a change of clothing in it? But I have checked his ticket; like our large friend, he is booked through to Margate. We'd better keep an eye those two. I'll warn my Southern colleague who comes on duty at Oxford for the Southern run."

"Yes," said Mr Hoyle. "We leave the train at Oxford, too. I'm meeting my sister there; it's been a year since she last saw my children, and then we travel on to Paddington for the children to see a pantomime. We return tomorrow."

"Well, thank you for your help, Mr Hoyle. You can leave the problem with me now; you've got your children to look after. I might see you tomorrow myself as well. I'm also returning on the Margate."

***

Back in their compartment, Mr Hoyle told Jimmy to keep a lookout from the corridor, and see if he saw either of the two men again on the platform at Banbury. He was to tell his father if one or both of them left the train. Jimmy obediently did what he was told – he would have been in the corridor anyway, to see which engines could be spotted in the station. But there were only a few passengers on the platform, and the two men were not among them. As for the engines, there was only a dirty old grey Hall class locomotive, clanking along and pulling a long rake of empty wagons slowly past on the down main line. Nothing of real railway interest that he could see. He had liked the station building at Leamington Spa, but this one at Banbury looked as if it could do with some major repair. The Leamington one looked sort of modern, and quite unlike the other stations on the line. He went back into the compartment and started to think of other things; it was not long before they would see their Aunty Doris again. Both children were very fond of their aunt, and they hadn't seen her for a long time.

***

As Guard Hewson went along the train, calling "Tickets, please!" and checking those of newly boarded passengers, he paused outside Charlton's compartment and gazed in to see whether anyone had boarded. Charlton looked uncomfortable. Why was the inspector taking so long? Surely he could see that nobody had entered since he was last here! The old man was paying no attention. He was keeping quiet, thought Charlton; but in spite of his appearance, he must have a First Class ticket, because the guard had checked it. By now, Charlton was quite certain that this was the same man who had caused him such grief at Wolverhampton. Well, there was the inkling of an idea sprouting in Charlton's mind, on how to foil whatever the bastard was planning. He had thought at the time that he had got shot of him there, but here the sod was again, right opposite! *Well, friend, you're in for a surprise,* mused Charlton. *You're going to leave the train at Oxford, and I'm not!*

Smiling to himself, he began to relax; the means of ridding himself of his unwelcome companion was becoming clear. The plan was risky, but if it worked then the pest would be gone for good.

Charlton noticed that his nemesis was dozing. He gently nudged his younger neighbour, muttering, "A word in private outside?"

Surprised but intrigued, the young man nodded.

"Follow me in about five minutes," Charlton whispered, and then got up.

At the end of the corridor, he waited, checking in his wallet and pulling out two five-pound notes. These he put into his pocket.

His neighbour appeared shortly after and asked, "You wanted something?"

"I do," replied Charlton. "D'you want to earn ten quid for doing practically nothing?"

The young man grinned. "I'm a lot younger than you, but I'm not stupid. That sounds risky."

"It's not at all risky. I need someone to take my case into a toilet for ten minutes at Oxford, and stay with it until I collect it again before we leave."

"That's all?"

"That's all."

"What's in the case?"

"What's in the case is not your business."

The young man gazed along the corridor for a moment and then slowly nodded. Charlton took a note out of his pocket and handed it over.

The young man examined it and stared at Charlton. "That's only five."

"There'll be another when I collect the case."

"Right." The young man returned to his seat and Charlton waited for a few more minutes before doing the same. The old fellow opposite was still asleep and obviously hadn't noticed anything. There was the chance of losing his money and the gun if the young man stole the case, of course, but Charlton's bank account could handle the loss; and he could equally easily warn the police that a young man was on the train, holding a case containing an illegal weapon. No, the chance of a loss was only slight. As the train paused in Banbury, Charlton remained seated, and showed no sign of getting up and leaving, so Wolseley made no move either; he had not yet thought of anything to sufficiently annoy Charlton into any form of action, so decided to let sleeping dogs lie.

***

As the train began to approach Oxford, Jimmy was out in the corridor on his observation duty once more but, as in Leamington and Banbury, there was nothing to report. This was disappointing, but Jimmy was not concerned; he knew that there would be far more of interest in Oxford. Not only would there be a change of engines, as in Wolverhampton, but this time the replacement would not be another GWR engine; it would belong to the Southern Railway, and it would be a different green altogether, or possibly even still black. He would have time during the changeover to have a good look at the new engine, as well as checking whether the two strange men did anything odd.

Jimmy was out in the corridor well before they arrived at the station platform, because he knew that before they arrived he would be able to get a quick view over on the left and catch a glimpse of the LMS line into Oxford at the Rewley Road station, which was only a branch to the LMS main line to the north, and then on to Cambridge, but was basically only a local line. Big passenger express engines were not normally to be seen there, unlike at its neighbour, which belonged to the GWR, and was on a main North-South route. You could even occasionally see LNER engines there, bringing trains from the north-east through Banbury. On top of all this, there was the meeting with Aunty Doris as well!

***

In Charlton's compartment, there was action. A subtle nudge from his shoulder had his young neighbour getting up and reaching for Charlton's case. Wolseley, watching through half-closed eyes, was startled to see the man take the case from the luggage rack and leave with it while Charlton just watched, unperturbed. What was this? Why on earth did Charlton not react to someone carrying his case? Had a switch perhaps been planned?

Charlton made a move to get up, put his coat on, and stepped out into the corridor. Perhaps he had asked the younger fellow to help him? Maybe they already knew each other. Wolseley decided he had better get ready to leave the train and follow Charlton. After all, he was the man Wolseley wanted.

By this time, Charlton was already in the corridor and leaving the train, as were quite a large number of passengers. But where was the fellow with Charlton's case? Were they both going to Margate? Wolseley could see Charlton's figure ahead, but there was no sign of the younger man. He worked his way into the crowd, as his prey disappeared into the booking hall and on towards the exit.

Once in the booking hall himself, Wolseley lost sight of Charlton and went outside into the street, but Charlton wasn't out there. Wolseley returned to the hall. Where the hell was he? Suddenly, Wolseley spotted him back on the platform; he must have hidden behind a luggage trolley, and Wolseley had missed him. *How in God's name could I have made such an elementary mistake?*

Wolseley raced back just in time to watch the train move off. He stood helpless on the platform. Charlton was standing in the corridor, waving cheerfully at him as the train swept past. Wolseley was furious with himself. He had been very neatly outsmarted! That hurt badly, but all was not lost: there would be another way to get to Margate.

***

Back on the train, Charlton went to the toilet and knocked on the door. It opened, and the young fellow passenger came out and gave him his case. The agreed second note was handed over.

Charlton didn't think the man would have had the necessary skills to open the case and steal any of the contents in the short time he had been in possession of it, and it was with great relief that he sat down in his seat. He had finally rid himself of whoever that was who had been plaguing him for the last four hours. Now he could enjoy the rest of his journey in peace, safe in the knowledge that his pursuer could not possibly catch him, because he didn't know where he was going. He would know the train was headed for Margate of course, but he wouldn't know whether Charlton was going all the way. Even if he did, he still wouldn't know where he would be staying!

Let's face it, thought Charlton, smiling to himself, *you're up against an expert. You don't stand a chance!*

CHAPTER 6

A Spoilt Meal

"Damn his eyes!" Wolseley swore as the train disappeared into the distance. Still, it could have been much worse; he knew where Charlton was heading to, and where he would be that evening, so all was not lost.

He stopped a passing porter. "Excuse me, when is the next train to Margate?"

"Margate? This time tomorrow. There's only one train a day. You'd be best served going to Paddington and getting across London to the Southern Railway. They'll have regular trains there, sir."

"Oh, then that's what I'll do. When is the next train to Paddington?"

"Er – in about fifteen minutes, sir, but you'll need a ticket. Your Margate ticket doesn't permit a change to a Paddington train."

"I'm very grateful to you, thank you."

Wolseley hurried to the booking office, bought a ticket to Paddington, then boarded the train. He was even able to relax in the buffet car, no longer having to keep a check on Charlton's whereabouts, so he enjoyed a leisurely lunch, before arriving in Paddington just after two o'clock.

In the information office, he borrowed a Bradshaw's timetable and found that a train left Waterloo for Margate shortly after four, and reached its destination before seven in the evening. He took the Underground to Waterloo Station, and purchased a ticket to Margate. He could have a late tea in the same hotel as Charlton, he mused, and give the man an extremely unpleasant surprise. He smiled to himself: that was something to look forward to. Revenge would be very sweet!

***

There had been a joyous meeting on the platform at Oxford, when Mr Hoyle and his children saw Aunty Doris waiting for them. The two children ran towards her as she recognised them and began to smile; she hadn't seen either of the children, or her brother, for many months. She had met with her brother from time to time during the wartime years, as he had travelled to Paddington on business, but had never been able to stay for long. The children hugged her, and they sat on a station bench together, while their aunt set down her basket and began to unpack various items.

She had, as expected, brought tea in a Thermos, as well as buns she had bought at the station cafeteria; she even had a packet of sweets for them.

"Share them nicely," she admonished, although

she was smiling, "and don't gobble them all before you get to Paddington! Keep some for later."

"Yes, Aunty," the children spoke in unison.

***

As the happy group sat and chatted amongst themselves, Fireman Hargreaves and Driver Denton walked past. They had been relieved by Oxford men who had taken their Star back to the Oxford shed for servicing, and the Southern engine (a King Arthur class, Jimmy had noted) had backed onto the train to take it further to Reading, and into Southern Railway territory to the South Coast.

"That looks like a happy family, Mr D," said Lance, after he and his driver had passed the group. "It's nice to see 'appy kids agen. P'raps we'll see some — Oh geez! Where's the bog?"

He hurried away, looking for the station toilet. George sighed.

A porter was standing looking at the tip a passenger had just given him and shaking his head sadly. Seeing George in his driver's clothing next to him, he grunted, "I used ter get a tanner, guaranteed, or even a shillin', but they on'y gives me a thrupenny bit these days."

"Yes, things will still be hard for a while. Can you tell me if there's a chemist near the station?"

"Chemist? Yeah, there's one about a 'undred yards towards the city on the left."

"Thanks," said George, and handed the man a coin.

"Here's another threepenny bit to make up your missing tanner."

"Coo, ta, guv'nor!" The porter's delighted smile cheered George up as he waited for his partner, who came up again after a few minutes. "Got there jus' in time, Mr D," gasped Lance.

"There's a chemist outside the station on the left," said George. "I suggest we pop in there for advice."

"Righto!"

The chemist knew exactly what was wanted, and provided the necessary. "Ta, Mr D," said Lance as they walked on to the enginemen's hostel where they would spend the night. "I'm lucky I've got a mate wot not on'y knows the road and signals through Oxford, but even knows where the bloody chemists are!"

"One does one's best," replied George modestly, omitting any mention of the porter's involvement.

***

On Oxford's main up platform, a grimy Grange class engine was pulling up with its ten empty coaches with the Paddington express. The family group gathered their bags, saying goodbye, and clambered onto the train. They found an empty compartment and the children both went back into the corridor to open the window and say a final few words to their aunt. The short stop in Oxford had been another very agreeable interlude on this exciting day out.

They continued waving while the train left the

station, quickly gathering speed, until Jimmy and May could no longer see their aunt, and they returned to their compartment.

"How long till we get to Paddington, Daddy?" asked Jimmy.

"Just over an hour, if we don't get a signal check."

"Then we go to the Lyons Corner House?" asked May swiftly.

Jimmy was annoyed: he had just been leading to that. What was it with girls that they always got in first?

"That's right," replied Mr Hoyle, opening the little Penguin paperback he had bought at the Oxford WHSmith bookstall.

But Jimmy's annoyance was again dissipated, by his interest in the Oxford marshalling yard they were passing, with its sidings of vans and trucks and shunting engines bustling to and fro.

It wasn't long before they were rounding a curve at Didcot and Jimmy was fascinated, as he observed the big shed on the right with its many locomotives, large and small; too many to note all their numbers, to his disappointment. Then there was Reading where, if you were lucky, you could catch a brief view of the small Southern Railway station on the right as you passed by. Jimmy was hardly on his seat at all as they ran along the Thames Valley; there was too much to see, especially as they approached the end of the line. He knew they were nearing London when he saw the Underground lines parallel to the main line, and caught sight of a low Underground train stopping at a station as they swept regally through at high speed. There was the huge shed at Old Oak Common; here you could even see Kings! A few minutes later, they passed Ranelagh Road servicing centre, where there were two more Kings, being readied for their next duties. Thoughts of annoying sisters, as well as of fathers and aunts, faded into the background, with all this fascinating railway scenery to observe.

Nevertheless, tea and the buns at Oxford were some time ago, and the Underground trip into the city brought them to the promised Lyons Corner House cafeteria, where the belated lunch overrode all expectations.

Replete now, Mr Hoyle took his two children to South Kensington to visit the Science Museum. Jimmy found the displays intriguing; especially the little models of suspension bridges destroyed by high winds. Both children were delighted by the enormous lightning flash from the suspended steel ball to the metal base in the demonstration, when several thousand volts were sent from the ball to the floor with a crack like thunder – which, in a sense, it was. A wonderful hour was spent in the museum, before it was time to head back for a quick bite and then queue up to enter the theatre to watch Dick Whittington with his cat overcome all odds and become Lord Mayor of London.

"Dick Whittington looks like a woman, Daddy," whispered May during the performance. Jimmy looked closely; his sister was right, the actor did look somehow female. Why was that? But these thoughts were driven out of his head by the hilarious clowning of the cat.

Sadly, the story came to its happy end, and they left the pantomime in pitch darkness and cold weather to catch a late Underground train to their hotel near Paddington Station. The weary children fell asleep instantly, while their father relaxed quietly over his book for half an hour, before he switched off the light and he too fell asleep.

***

When he had reached the hotel at Margate, Charlton had opened the door to his room, placed his case on the bed, and locked the door. He knew there was no real reason to do this, because he had left his pursuer fuming on the platform in Oxford – a matter which still provoked smiles of immense satisfaction. But he was a believer in 'belt and braces' in matters of his personal safety.

He unpacked his case, lifted his clean shirt, and stared in horror at the space where his first five hundred pounds should have been. All the money was missing! He scrabbled rapidly underneath the underwear, and sighed with relief when he saw the second bundle of notes; the thief must have missed those. Then he searched down the side, to discover his gun was also missing. *That swine in the toilet with my case!* he raged. *He must have helped himself to my gun as well as helping me to trick that old bastard!*

There was no earthly use going to the police: he could hardly claim his gun back – there would be very difficult questions to answer, and he had no idea where, or who, his so-called helper was anyway. A clear description to the police would not help; the sod would be miles away by now.

With his remaining five hundred pounds, at least he could pay his hotel bill; depending, of course, how long he proposed to stay. With that consideration, he shut and locked his case, and determined to go downstairs to the dining room to enjoy his evening meal. Nobody was going to stop Benjamin Charlton from relishing the Dover sole and new potatoes he could see on the menu! Then there was steamed pudding to follow, with a cup of coffee and a cigar. He could mull with pleasure over his next few days of ease, while that nameless old bugger was chasing around the south of England in vain, wondering where his prey was.

***

The train from Waterloo arrived at Margate on time, and Wolseley got up to grab his haversack from the luggage rack. On leaving the station, he asked the ticket inspector whether he could direct him to the hotel he knew Charlton had booked into.

"Sorry sir, no, I can't help you; I don't know that hotel. But there is usually a policeman on point duty, directing traffic on the main street, about fifty yards down the road. He might know."

Wolseley thanked him and left the station, heading down the road until he saw the policeman, with whom he had more success.

"Yes, sir. That street's about five minutes away, down this road and the first on the right. The hotel is about thirty yards along the left-hand side of the road. You can't miss it."

The well-used phrase was often an exaggeration or even a lie, Wolseley knew, but in this case the policeman was correct, and Wolseley found the hotel within ten minutes. He entered just before seven, and booked a room for himself for the night; he didn't expect to stay longer.

As he climbed the stairs, he glanced through the open restaurant door and saw Charlton sitting there, tucking into his main course, unaware that in a few minutes his appetite was going to be ruined by someone he was definitely not expecting to see again – and certainly not in this hotel.

Wolseley carried on up the stairs to his room, took his coat off, and laid it on the bed. The room was plain but clean, and entirely satisfactory for what he had planned. He had been awake for two days now, aside from a couple of naps seized at times when he thought nothing would happen, but such situations had often occurred during his career, and he thought he could still manage. He sat and considered his options for a few moments; he was in two minds about whether to go down now and spoil Charlton's dinner, or whether to wait until the middle of the night and then enter the man's room and deal with him in private. But suppose somehow Charlton inadvertently caught sight of him in the hotel, and spoiled the shock of his sudden appearance?

Despite the draw of the bed, Wolseley was very hungry, and realised that he hadn't eaten properly since he was in the buffet car on the Paddington train. Mind made up, he made his way down to the hotel's restaurant, with a pleasant smile on his face. He strode in and aimed for a table next to where his quarry was sitting.

"Evening, Benjamin," he murmured, as he walked past the man, and sat down at the table, where Charlton could see him clearly.

***

Benjamin Charlton had relished his fish and was halfway through the steamed pudding, wishing he could eat like this every day. The hotel cook must be a master chef, he was thinking, as he dug his spoon into another piece of the pudding and lifted it towards his mouth. *What the fuck?* That old bastard from the train passed his table, greeting him by name, and then sat at a nearby table, in brazen plain sight. Charlton dropped his spoon and serviette, jumped up, and hurried out of the restaurant, up to his room.

He sat on his bed, his mind in a total frenzy. *How in the name of all that's holy has the bugger got to Margate and found out which hotel I'm staying in? How on earth has he discovered my name? Is that bastard Smith involved in this? By God, if he is, I'll drop him right in it;*

I could tell the police a great deal about our Mr Smith.

But a far more immediate question was uppermost in his mind: what the hell was he to do now? It was time for action of some sort – serious action. He would have almost gone back to the restaurant and shot the bleeder, if he'd still had his gun, but of course, that would have had him in a noose within weeks. No. He would have to think rationally, and produce a far more effective solution – and quickly!

CHAPTER 7

A Confession near Banbury

Roger Wolseley grinned as he saw Charlton's reaction to his arrival in the restaurant; he knew panic when he saw it. After Charlton hurried out, Wolseley left his own table and went out into the reception area, picked up the haversack he had left there, paid his bill, and left the hotel. Now all he had to do was to wait.

He sauntered out, to watch unobtrusively from across the road, and see whether Charlton would try to sneak out and search for another hotel. A few minutes later, his patience was rewarded; Charlton scurried out, carrying his suitcase, and looked carefully around just as Wolseley ducked out of sight. Satisfied that his pursuer was nowhere in sight, Charlton set off along the road.

Following him was relatively easy in the dark, and Charlton was clearly not as well practised in avoiding surveillance as he ought to have been. Wolseley had taken the precaution of bringing his haversack with him, so he didn't need to go back to fetch it, and could simply book in at whichever hotel

Charlton found. Margate in winter was a quiet resort, and Charlton very soon found another hotel. He gazed around once more before he entered and, having seen nothing threatening, booked himself in for the night.

Wolseley waited for half an hour before entering the same hotel and taking a room. He assumed that Charlton would not visit the restaurant, as he had already eaten; he would almost certainly stay in his room. Wolseley asked if a simple snack could be sent up for himself, as he didn't want to risk being spotted in the hotel if this could be avoided.

"And I have another small request," he said to the clerk. "I believe a friend of mine has booked in. A Mr Charlton. Could you tell me which room he has?" The clerk told him and Wolseley thanked him, adding, "It's a bit late, so I won't disturb him now. I'll catch up with him at breakfast."

Wolseley went to his own room and sat on the bed, opened his haversack, and took out a sheet of paper. He paused for a moment or two, thinking about how he could best create another reaction from Charlton. He wrote a few words on the paper, folded it neatly, and left his room again, returning two minutes later.

***

Charlton was quite sure that he had eluded his pursuer; even so, as before, he locked his door carefully, pushing the back of a chair under the doorknob for extra security, and then he sat down.

Opening his case, he took out his pyjamas and got himself dressed for bed. It had been a day full of excitement and, he admitted to himself, apprehension. But that was all going to change. If that blighter came again, Charlton would head back to Chester and call his two enforcers. He had no doubt that for ten quid each they would be able to handle an elderly fellow and make clear to the man that poking his nose into Charlton's life was a guaranteed method of gaining a lengthy stay in hospital. He was even tempted to consider a more permanent solution, if the man proved stubborn; fifty pounds each should be adequate for that, he thought grimly. It would ensure that any further difficulties would be rendered completely impossible.

While he was mulling over these matters, he heard a strange slithering sound, as if something was sliding on the floor. He glanced around in curiosity; he hadn't felt any kind of draught, and the window had been firmly shut – he'd made sure of that – and the hotel did not seem to be the sort that would harbour rats or other vermin; the room had cost enough. He heard the sound again and looked towards the door with increasing fear. The corner of what appeared to be a folded note could be seen. Trembling, he bent to pick it up and unfolded it. It was quite short: *Did you really think I couldn't find you?*

Charlton was normally proud of his ability to keep his temper, but this was too much. His fear metamorphosed into a deep and cold fury. He would return to Chester on the next train, and call his two thugs as soon as he got home; it would be well worth a hundred pounds to get this bastard off his tail permanently. In the meantime, he was going to sleep, have his breakfast in the morning, and if the bugger was also there, well sod him. He was not going to plague Benjamin Charlton for much longer!

As he was mentally committing himself to this topic, he decided to get Smith to organise another gun for him. While it was unlikely that the two thugs would fail him – they never had before – extra security was always to be considered. A quick phone call would be all that was necessary.

That night, Charlton's sleep was disturbed by dreams of running and hiding, only to see the hated figure popping up. It was almost with relief that he woke, dressed, and went down to breakfast; he was surprised not to see his pursuer already there. The man had definitely been in the hotel, so why had he not appeared in order to taunt Charlton? No matter – he would not be annoying him much longer; Charlton's thugs or Smith would see to that!

Charlton finished his breakfast, went to his room to pack, paid his bill, and set off for the station. The train for Chester and Birkenhead was due to leave at a quarter past nine.

On the platform, Charlton carefully studied the waiting passengers, but again there was no sign of the elderly man. This was puzzling. Charlton boarded the train and spent the few minutes before departure staring out of the window, to see whether the man would board at the last minute, but there was no sign of him at all. Since the train began here in Margate, he could not be on board already. With luck, the bugger had overslept.

***

From his own room, Wolseley heard Charlton creeping out; he slipped to his door, opening it very slightly to see that his prey had no case, and was therefore not leaving yet. He guessed that the man would be planning to leave soon after breakfast, and would probably return to Chester as soon as he could. Wolseley decided to do the same, but did not want Charlton to see him. He estimated that Charlton would take about twenty minutes at least to finish his breakfast, so he gave the man time to settle and order his egg and bacon, then he left the hotel and made his way to the station.

A brief perusal of the local timetable showed him that the daily through train from Margate to Birkenhead left at nine-fifteen, so there was plenty of time for him to grab a snack in the station cafeteria. But then, he reasoned, Charlton would see him board the train.

He checked the timetable once more, to find that he could take the 8.17 to Ramsgate and board the Birkenhead train there. Charlton might not be watching for him. This would also give him time for a cup of tea and a bun or two in the station canteen.

Wolseley caught the earlier train and went to the

cafeteria in Ramsgate as planned, thoroughly enjoying his snack, then he searched for a dark corner on the platform, where he waited as the through train for Birkenhead came in. He noticed Charlton sitting at a window seat, gazing casually at the boarding passengers. Luckily, there were enough people for Wolseley to slip easily among them at the rear of the train, where he climbed into the last coach, fairly certain that he couldn't have been spotted.

Relaxing in his seat, he took stock of his situation, and finally settled for leaving Charlton in blissful ignorance of his presence, until they reached Reading or Oxford after lunch. Then he would spring his little surprise and see what eventuated from Charlton's reaction. The only problem he might need to prepare for was the possibility of Charlton coming through the train to check the compartments himself. However, Lady Luck appeared to be on Wolseley's side, as the train was quite full, and many passengers were standing in the corridors. Wolseley did not believe that his target would bother to work his portly way past so many people, so with confidence he simply sat back to survey the landscape of Kent; the 'Garden of England', as the inhabitants proudly called it.

Wolseley stayed in his seat as the train passed Canterbury, Ashford and Redhill; he was quite sure that Charlton would stay on the train all the way back to Chester, unless something unexpected happened. Between Reading and Didcot, he got up, grabbed his haversack, and went into the toilet. Here, he took out Charlton's automatic and a handkerchief, wetted the handkerchief in the washbasin, and rubbed his own prints thoroughly off the gun. He took a pair of gloves from his bag and put them on. It was a cold winter's day, so he was sure the gloves wouldn't excite comment. Wolseley slid the gun into his pocket; he had no intention of firing it, but it paid to be prepared with someone like this particular criminal. He hadn't checked the man's case thoroughly on the previous day's journey, and couldn't be sure that another gun wasn't hidden there, unlikely though that seemed.

***

After a traditional and filling breakfast the following morning, Mr Hoyle took both children across to city to Gamages, the renowned toyshop in Regent Street. Each child was given a florin, and told to choose what they wanted. May looked at doll's dresses and Jimmy shot straight to the toy trains. May soon returned with a small parcel containing a dress she had bought for her doll, but Jimmy returned empty-handed.

"Didn't you find what you wanted, Jimmy?" asked his father.

"Yes, Dad, but it cost three and six, so I'm going to save the two shillings you gave me and save up for the rest so that I can buy the van I want."

His father nodded. "Well done, Jimmy. You are acting wisely, I'm pleased to see."

It was now time to take the Tube back to the hotel, pick up their bags, and walk to Paddington to catch the Oxford train. It would give them an hour to wait and once again a chance to catch up with their aunt, before the connecting train from Margate could take them all back home.

***

Near the front of the train, in his First Class compartment, Charlton was much more at ease. He had studied the passengers boarding with him at Margate, and had seen no sign of his pursuer. Presumably he had fooled him with his early departure from the hotel. He had even had a quick lookout at Ramsgate and Dover too, but had seen nothing suspicious. He had tried to check the whole train, and had walked along the corridors of two coaches, but had been annoyed by the indignant grunts of passengers standing in the corridors. In the third coach, a young workman (judging by his clothing) had stood in his way, and refused to move.

"If ye're goin' ter the bog, mate, go back. Ye're not pushin' past me! Bugger off back ter yer own seat!"

"No need to be coarse, young fellow!" But Charlton was not keen on fisticuffs if they could be avoided, and he turned and went back. The train was quite long and to get anywhere he would have had to force his way past many passengers in corridors. In any case, he recalled, it was that turd who had walked the corridors yesterday, not him. They had now passed Didcot and were approaching Oxford. Only four more hours to reach home, then he could get on the phone to Smith and the two enforcers. Between the four of them, they would soon get the bleeder off his tail!

Casually, Charlton studied the platform crowd as the train paused at Oxford, but the old man did not show himself, and shortly afterwards, Charlton allowed himself to have a snooze. Some time later, he was woken by a gentle nudge from his neighbour. "It seems that a gentleman in the corridor would like a word with you."

Charlton, still sleepy, looked towards the corridor and was horrified to see his hated antagonist, crooking his finger at him!

"If I were you, I'd go and see what he wants," recommended the neighbour.

"Ye-er, yes," stuttered Charlton, and he got up slowly, easing the sliding door open. He reluctantly joined Wolseley in the corridor.

"What in hell's name do you want with me, you bastard?" he snarled.

"Just a short conversation," replied Wolseley. "Let's go to the end of the coach, where we can talk without being disturbed. No-one will gather there until we are nearing Banbury."

He began to move, with Charlton unwillingly following. They reached the end of the coach and turned to the door there.

"Have a look out," offered Wolseley.

Charlton did so. "What am I looking for?"

"Nothing," responded Wolseley, holding him tightly against the wall, while he pulled the door open so that his prisoner could see the hedgerow flashing past less than fifteen inches away from his frightened gaze.

"I need a simple answer to a simple question," said Wolseley conversationally. "Who provided you with the lethal component to add to the medication you sold to the hospitals; killing, to my certain knowledge, at least five patients?"

"I can't tell you that!" gasped Charlton, suddenly feeling a hard pressure on the base of his spine.

"Oh, I think you can," replied Wolseley firmly, "otherwise this gun of yours will go off, and your corpse will fall out of the train."

"I can't tell you the man's name!" stuttered Charlton. "He'll kill me!" He had no doubt whatsoever about that; Smith was a cold-hearted bastard.

"I expect he would. But if you give me the information I want, I might not."

"Someone'd hear the shot!" Charlton cried in desperation.

"Probably," replied Wolseley, "but by the time they got here, there'd be no body, no gun, and the door would be shut. There'd be nothing suspicious to see at all."

"You wouldn't dare kill me!"

"You're running out of time, Benjamin. I'll count to three. One…"

"Your fingerprints will be on the gun!" Charlton was shaking in fright.

"I'm wearing gloves. Two…"

"Smith! Walter Smith!" spat out Charlton and even gave Wolseley Smith's phone number. If the bugger got Smith off his tail, Charlton would actually feel easier, he realised; then he could still see his two other men and sort out this bastard.

"Thank you," said Wolseley and, slamming the door shut, he released Charlton from his grip. "Don't forget that I know where you live, and I will be visiting if that number is false."

On the way back to his seat, Wolseley saw a lady coming towards him, apparently heading for the toilet. As she eased past him, he slipped the gun into her open handbag, with neither her agreement nor knowledge. A shaking Charlton scurried back to his compartment, fervently hoping that Wolseley would get to Smith before the latter could find out who shopped him. Sitting in his seat, he had an idea; what if he contacted the police at the next station? They would search Wolseley, find the gun, and arrest the bugger for illegal possession of a firearm! That would give him time to organise a more permanent solution.

***

At the end of the platform in Banbury, Driver Denton and Fireman Hargreaves were waiting to relieve the London Division enginemen off the Margate train.

Lance noticed a father with two children waiting further down the platform.

"I think those kids were on our train yesterday, Mr D," he remarked.

"Oh yes?" said George absentmindedly; he was wondering about yesterday's difficulty in the cab. "And are you over your physical embarrassment now, Lance? Or do I have to worry about the state of my tender again today?"

"No, I'm fine now, Mr D. Them pills—"

"*Those* pills," muttered George.

"*Those* pills worked fine, and – 'ey up, 'ere's our train."

As the Margate train pulled slowly in, the driver was leaning out of the cab, and when he saw the two relief crewmen waiting, a wide grin spread over his face. George looked in surprise at the number on the buffer beam of the oncoming engine. "That's not one of ours, Lance," he remarked. "It's an Oxford engine, and they'll want it back again smartly. This'll probably mean an engine change at Wolverhampton."

The driver brought the locomotive to a stop, and applied the brake. "George Denton!" he said, as the replacement crew climbed into the cab. "Haven't seen you for years, mate. How're things?"

A responding smile spread over George's face as he recognised an earlier colleague. "Good lord! Reg Bilsom! I heard you'd retired years ago, Reg."

"Yes, I did, but in '39 I re-joined for the Duration. They were suddenly short of experienced drivers."

George and Lance climbed into the cab of the Castle class locomotive, and the four men exchanged greetings and details about the condition of the engine, before the Oxford men climbed down.

"Reg gave me a lot of encouragement when I came back from the first war, Lance," explained George as his fireman looked out of the cab for the guard's signal to start.

***

On the platform, May and Jimmy climbed into the train with their father, before settling down in their seats. The two days had been very exciting, but now they were rather tired, and ready for a snooze; although Jimmy feared he might miss engines that he wouldn't normally see. Nevertheless, his eyelids began to droop, and he was soon fast asleep, like May.

Mr Hoyle was pleased that his children had enjoyed their little excursion, and seeing their aunt again. Once he was sure that they were dozing, he too closed his eyes for a while. *Now it's my turn for a quiet hour's snooze,* he thought to himself.

He was wrong.

CHAPTER 8

Contretemps at Birmingham

The starting signal cleared the route, the guard's green flag was waved, and the two enginemen started their train on the run to Chester, where they would book off. Their Castle class locomotive was in reasonable condition. Reg had told George it had not shown any problems on the run from Reading.

"Should be an easy run then, without any loss of time, Mr D," Lance remarked.

George agreed, and so it seemed until they arrived in Leamington Spa.

"Wot the 'ell?" called Lance, spotting two policemen on the main down platform of Leamington's Great Western station as he was watching the passengers (for any young, attractive females, it must be admitted). The policemen were talking to a portly man, who was gesturing to the rear of the train. The three men were joined by the guard, and all four boarded the train.

"Problem, Lance?" asked George as he came over to Lance's side of the cab and looked out along the platform.

"We've got coppers on the train!" said Lance in dismay. "This'll lose us time. An' we won't be able to make it up until after 'hampton." He looked again, "An' that fat bloke with the coppers is the one wot ran inter me on the platform at Snow 'ill, yesterday!"

It was in fact a further twenty minutes before the police left the train and the guard signalled for the departure once more.

***

In his seat near the rear of the train, with passengers boarding and leaving, Wolseley was fuming, as he saw Charlton arriving with two policemen and the train guard. "That's the man!" said Charlton in the corridor, excitedly pointing him out to the policemen.

"Come into the corridor please, sir," said one of them to Wolseley. Wolseley got up and joined them as requested.

"What can I do for you gentlemen?" he asked, wondering what madness Charlton was engaged in this time; this did not seem like a panic. The man had what appeared to be a smug expression on his face.

"Are you carrying a gun, sir?" asked one of the policemen.

"Of course not!" said Wolseley indignantly. "Why on earth would I be carrying a gun?"

"If you don't mind, sir," said the other constable, moving to him and swiftly patting him down in a manner which Wolseley recognised as very professional; this copper missed nothing.

The constable looked at his colleague. "He's clean, Bert."

The first constable looked at Charlton. "I think this is a case of mistaken identity, sir," he told him, then turned to Wolseley. "We're very sorry to have disturbed you."

The police and the guard left the train without further ado. Charlton glared angrily at Wolseley, and also left.

Wolseley had assumed he had put the fear of God into Charlton, yet the man had called the police, hoping to have him arrested with the gun on his person. He had intended to leave him to stew for the rest of the journey, yet Charlton had not been as frightened as he ought to have been. It was clearly time to reinforce that fear. At least he now knew for sure that Charlton did not have a gun; the police would have been very careful to pat him down as well as Wolseley himself. Second-hand guns were relatively common after the end of the war, kept as souvenirs, but many had strayed into criminal hands, as Wolseley knew from talking to some of his ex-colleagues. Even so, they were still not common in criminal undertakings; Britain had not yet succumbed to the plague that had taken over America since Prohibition had given the Mafia such an unending supply of wealth, now a major source of power and influence in the big crime syndicates there. Even with the ending of Prohibition, the gangs were now so well entrenched that it was almost impossible to deal effectively with them. Al Capone himself, once the most wanted man in the United States, had only been caught through a careless tax infringement. The police had been unable to charge him with the murders and other crimes he had been guilty of. Witnesses had either all suffered from curiously unreliable memories, or mysterious deaths.

***

Mr Hoyle had woken from his pleasant doze during the wait in Leamington, and was sitting quietly with his children, both now also awake, when the guard popped his head inside. "Could I trouble you for a moment, Mr Hoyle?" he asked. Mr Hoyle saw that his children were occupied; May with her doll and Jimmy with a railway magazine. He nodded and went into the corridor to join the guard.

"What's up, Gordon?"

"We've had a little trouble in the train again," said the guard, "and I thought you should be aware of the details. It concerns the two gentlemen we saw on this train yesterday. They're both back today, and are already causing trouble. The portly gent accused the older man of carrying a gun, and he called the police at Leamington."

"Good heavens! Ah – that's why we were late departing. I did wonder."

"Yes. But since nothing incriminating, and no gun, could be found, the police let everyone go."

"What, both men from yesterday are on the train again today?"

"Yes, they are."

"Where are they travelling to?"

"Both have tickets back to Chester."

"Damn," Mr Hoyle sighed. "Gordon, we can't do anything if there's no evidence, but that doesn't mean we can't keep a close eye on the pair of them. I'm afraid that's going to be largely your job, but I'll back you up if there's any further problem. Don't worry about that."

"Thank you, Mr Hoyle. It's nice to have authority behind me. But this little discussion with the police might have settled the pair down. Let's hope the rest of the journey will be quiet and peaceful."

Guard Hewson's hope was to be dashed before they reached Snow Hill Station. Sitting in his office in the brake-van, he saw a rather worried lady standing by his open door. She was wiping her eyes with her handkerchief.

"Yes, madam, can I help you?" he asked.

"I sincerely hope so," she said. "When I reached into my handbag just now, to take out my handkerchief, I found a… a gun. It certainly wasn't there when I got on the train," she began to cry, "and I don't want the horrible thing!"

"Goodness me! Look, I'll take it from you," said the guard. "Er – have you touched it at all?"

"Good gracious, no; I wouldn't dare!"

Guard Hewson took out his handkerchief and lifted the gun gingerly out of the lady's handbag, making sure that his own fingerprints were not imprinted on the weapon. He wrapped it in a spare red flag from the flag locker. "We'll have the police look into this, madam, when we stop in Birmingham in a few minutes," he said, "but they will want your full details. Have some evidence of your identity ready for them in Snow Hill."

As he spoke, he saw that they were already in the tunnel just south of the station and added, "We'll be stopping in a moment or two. Please get your case and return here with it for the police to talk to you."

The lady nodded gratefully, then left to return with her suitcase and wait in the guard's van.

As the train pulled up, Gordon Hewson dropped to the platform and waved urgently to a nearby platform inspector. The man came over.

"Hello Gordon, what's the problem?"

"We need the railway police urgently, sir. We have a problem with three passengers, and a handgun."

The inspector nodded and hurried away, returning quickly with a uniformed constable and a sergeant.

"That was quick!" commented Guard Hewson in surprise.

"Yes," replied the sergeant. "Leamington police were on the phone to us ten minutes ago, warning us about a passenger, possibly with a gun."

"Yes, there is a gun; it's quite safe. I've got it," said Gordon Hewson. "A passenger found it in her handbag, and I took it from her for safe-keeping. She's in my van now, Sergeant."

***

In the cab, a disbelieving Lance glared down the platform. "I don't bloody believe it, Mr D!" he snapped. "There's coppers on the platform agen, talking to Mr Hewson!"

George Denton closed his eyes in anger. "Blast! We're already down twenty minutes; it's going to take serious efforts to make up time." Lance stared at his driver in shock; in almost ten years of firing to the man, he had very rarely heard him swear. What was this? They had often been held up in the war, sometimes for hours; this was only a twenty-minute delay. Why the bloody language?

"Sorry, Lance," George Denton apologised, "I had hoped we'd be home on time. I promised Alice I would take her to the pictures tonight at the Odeon, to celebrate her birthday."

"I bet it's to do with that fat sod wot nearly ran me down on the platform yesterday."

"Well, let's hope the police sort the lot of them out quickly, and allow us get on with our jobs," growled George angrily.

***

There was also excitement in Jimmy Hoyle's compartment: the boy had caught sight of the police on the platform.

"Hey Dad, there are some policemen on the platform talking to Mr Hewson." He had heard his father mention the guard's name.

Mr Hoyle looked up with a sigh; he suspected that

he might have to get involved once more. "I'd better go to speak to the guard again," he grumbled, and as Jimmy got up to come with him, he added, "No, you stay here, Jimmy, and look after May."

Why is it always me who has to look after May? thought a frustrated Jimmy. He wanted to see what was going on. Sometimes, it was very irritating being a small boy.

In the guard's van, the two policemen were inspecting the gun, which the guard was holding in his handkerchief. The lady who had found it was explaining the circumstances, relating how the gun must have been slipped into her handbag as she was passing somebody in the corridor on her way to the toilet. She did not recall anyone passing her, however. The sergeant nodded, but when he saw Mr Hoyle entering, he began, "Excuse me, sir, this is a private matter, and we—"

"No, Sergeant; this is Mr Hoyle," explained Guard Hewson quickly. "He is a senior railway official, who I am very thankful to have on the train. He knows all the details."

"Ah, I see," said the sergeant. "Could you find the two men who were seen by our colleagues in Leamington, please? We need to interview them quickly if the train is to continue."

"Certainly; they are still on the train, as far as I know. They both have tickets for Chester." The guard hurried away into the corridor.

"It's my understanding, Mr Hoyle, that Guard Hewson is actually in charge of the train, and it cannot continue until he gives the signal. Is that correct?" asked the sergeant.

"Yes," replied Mr Hoyle, "that's quite correct; even I couldn't override his authority on this train."

"Well, you must know, sir, that we will have to satisfy ourselves that nobody is in any danger before we can allow this train to continue," the sergeant stated.

"Yes, I'm fully aware of that, Sergeant, and I—" What he was going to say halted as the guard entered the office again, accompanied by both Wolseley and Charlton, the latter appearing to be very angry.

"This is harassment," spluttered Charlton. "I shall have a great deal to say to my lawyer, when I get home. You can be sure that I will contact him immediately on my return this afternoon!"

"You are, of course, welcome to do that, sir, but that depends rather on whether you will be allowed home today." The police sergeant was untroubled by Charlton's bluster. He glanced at his constable. "Pat 'em both down, Charlie. You know what we're looking for." The constable did as he was bid then, looking at his sergeant, shook his head.

The sergeant looked again at Charlton. "We can deal with the matter here on the train quietly and sensibly, sir, or alternatively we can go to the police office here at Snow Hill. If all our questions are answered to our satisfaction, then we shall naturally release you to catch the next train to Chester. Which would you prefer, sir?"

"Ask your damn questions, then."

The sergeant looked at Wolseley, who said, "Might I have a quiet word with you, Sergeant, perhaps in the corridor? I think it would save us all a great deal of time."

"Very good, sir," replied the sergeant and led the way. "Now, what did you want to tell me?"

"I am ex-Detective Inspector Wolseley of the Chester City Police, very recently retired. I have been following Mr Charlton in the hope of gaining evidence against him for his criminal black-market activities during the war. So far, I must confess, without success. I suspect him of having been armed with a weapon, possibly a handgun."

"I see, sir, and have you any documentation to prove who you are?"

"As you must know, I handed my warrant back when I retired. I only have my driving licence now; but you can call the Chester police, and ask for Chief Superintendent Henderson. He will confirm my identity."

"Thank you, Mr Wolseley, we will do that." They returned to the guard's office, where the sergeant directed his constable to search Charlton again.

"What – what are you doing, Officer?" Charlton was furious at being patted all over.

"Just checking, sir." The constable looked at his sergeant and shook his head. "Nothing, Sarge."

The police spent a few minutes questioning the two men, and then the lady who had handed the gun in, but finding nothing they could hold anybody on, they kept the gun, and allowed the train to continue. Wolseley was annoyed that no fingerprints had been taken but knew that the grounds for such a procedure were too weak.

On their way back to their respective seats, Charlton passed Wolseley and muttered, "I hope you've got a good escape plan from Chester; you're going to bloody need one!"

***

In the cab, George pulled out his watch, grunting, "Good job we're outside the overall roof, Lance, we've had to blow off some steam."

Engine drivers were generally banned from allowing their engines to blow off steam under cover. "And I hope the long break has relaxed your shoulders, lad; we're going to have to try and make up plenty of time. We're now fifty-five minutes late."

"You can rely on me, Mr D. I'm champin' at the bit. Wot's a bit, any'ow?"

"You're not a racing man, I see, Lance. The bit is that part of a horse's equipment that fits in its mouth, so when a horse is champing at the bit, it's keen to get moving again."

"So that's it. Seems a bit daft that a 'orse wot wants to run should chomp on a bit of metal across its gob. No accountin' fer taste, I say."

George chuckled, thankful that his fireman had a good sense of humour, even if his language left a lot to be desired. Unfortunately, there was little chance of picking up much time between Birmingham and Wolverhampton; this was a very busy stretch of the main line, with speed limits.

Only after Wolverhampton, with a reduced load, could they hope to try and make up time, having detached four coaches there. Fast running was only really possible after leaving Shrewsbury, and even then the hilly run could hamper speeds; George wished he had one of the new County class locomotives instead of their Castle. The new engines could run out of steam up the hills but could pick it up again very quickly on the downhill runs; they were ideal for the hilly stretches with moderate loads.

***

Further back in the train, three other men were equally deep in thought. Charlton was wondering how he was going to shake off his pursuer, and what method of destruction he would choose to ensure the man could cause him no further annoyance in the future. Wolseley was reviewing a number of possible methods he could employ to irritate Charlton and drive him into some precipitate, and consequently inadvisable, action, which would allow Wolseley to checkmate him. The third man was Mr Hoyle, who was wondering what new aggravation the two men could cause to worry him and the guard, and disturb his children before they all reached Chester.

The three men didn't have long to wait; the train was due into Wolverhampton in under twenty minutes.

CHAPTER 9

A Message from Shrewsbury

Mr Hoyle decided to play safe and walk along the corridor, to see what the other two men were up to, so that he could perhaps interfere with any further planned disturbance. He passed them both, in their separate compartments, and they appeared to be quiet, although Charlton glared at him as he went past. Wolseley paid him no attention.

Hoyle carried on, to speak briefly to Gordon Hewson and suggest that they both keep a sharp eye out at Wolverhampton, where the train would pause to allow the rear four coaches to be detached. Oddly, the station at Wolverhampton Low Level was not as busy as Mr Hoyle had expected, and the wait was without any undue incident. Both troublesome men had presumably decided to call a truce, he thought. The coaches were detached, and the train left again without further delay.

***

As soon as the train left the station, Guard Hewson began his walk along its corridors once more, to check the tickets of those passengers who had just boarded. On his return, he met Mr Hoyle.

"All quiet on the Great Western front this time, Gordon?"

"Yes, Mr Hoyle, they're both quiet as little mice. I notice too that Driver Denton is beginning to pick up the pace."

Indeed, the train's speed had noticeably increased.

"Trying to make up lost time," agreed Mr Hoyle. "With any luck, those two passengers will give us some peace until we reach Chester. Do you come off duty there, Gordon, or are you going through to Woodside?" Woodside was the Birkenhead terminus.

"No, I come off at Chester, thank goodness."

"Right, well let me know if there's any more trouble. We seem to have fewer passengers now," said Mr Hoyle, and he returned to his children.

***

Wolseley had also noticed that the train had fewer passengers, and he felt it was time to check on his target once more, to see if the man appeared to be planning anything untoward. He decided it would be best to do this without Charlton knowing he was being observed. When he arrived at Charlton's First Class compartment, he was surprised to see that the man was missing, and that the only other passenger there was asleep. Very gently, Wolseley slid the door open, reached for the luggage rack, and eased

Charlton's case down, before leaving with it and moving two coaches back. He entered an empty toilet and locked the door, then took his little device out and opened the locked case once more, this time thoroughly checking its contents. He found a second pack of notes he had missed the first time he'd had the case, and slipped them into his pocket. Then he locked the case and left the toilet. Going to the nearest door, he lifted the strap to open the window and threw the case out, before shutting the window again and returning to his seat.

Let's see what he does about that!

He didn't have long to wait; a furious Charlton appeared at his compartment five minutes later. He was raging. "What have you done with my bloody case, you sod?"

"Case? What case?" Wolseley was all innocence.

"I know you've stolen it!"

"Stolen your case? What would be the point of that? Anyway, if I had come in and taken your case, your fellow passengers would have seen me."

"There was only one, and the stupid bugger fell asleep!" Charlton's face was red with anger.

"Surely he would have heard me opening the sliding door?"

"Don't give me that! You slid the door open gently; he wouldn't have heard anything."

"Anyway, what makes you think I've stolen your case?"

"Because you've been hounding me for two bloody days, that's why!"

Wolseley stood up and glared at Charlton. "Now look here! You've had the police on me twice already. We'll be in Wellington soon, and if you call the coppers a third time and explain how I have stolen your case, I will inform them how you have already called the police twice today. What did they conclude? Tell me that!"

"You wriggled out of both occasions; you know you did!"

"What you have done all along is to make a nuisance of yourself, both to me and to the police." Wolseley felt Charlton's temperature going up, and wanted to increase the pressure on the man. "That's called harassment, I believe; and it's an offence. You really want that?"

Charlton snorted in disgust and left, slamming the door closed as he did so.

***

It was Jimmy who had noticed the case. "Hey, Dad, did you just see a suitcase fly past the window?" he asked in surprise.

Mr Hoyle looked up from his paper. "A suitcase?" he queried, eyebrows raised.

"I'm sure it was, Dad. It landed in a field."

God Almighty! Mr Hoyle groaned mentally as he got up. "I'd better go and see the guard again," he said to Jimmy. "You must—"

"Yes I know, Dad, keep an eye on May," sighed Jimmy.

May was busy changing her doll's clothes. "You've got your dress dirty, you naughty girl. How did you do that?" She changed a perfectly clean doll's dress for another perfectly clean dress. She was not interested in what her menfolk did or said. *Dolls were like small children: you had to keep looking after them and make sure they behaved themselves and didn't get into trouble.*

Mr Hoyle walked carefully along the train again, but the compartment where he had previously seen Charlton was empty, apart from a sleeping passenger. There was no sign of a suitcase in the rack above Charlton's empty seat, either. He winced; it seemed that something was amiss once more. Hurrying on to where he knew Wolseley had been sitting, he met an angry Charlton, who was seemingly returning to his seat. Hoyle nodded to him. "All in order?" Charlton merely grunted as they passed. *Apparently not,* decided Mr Hoyle, but he said nothing.

Wolseley was sitting quietly in his seat, reading a paperback, but he looked up as he saw Mr Hoyle. "Hello again, something wrong?"

"Er – no. I just passed Mr Charlton in the corridor. He seemed annoyed about something, and I wondered if he had been pestering you again, Mr Wolseley?"

"He came to accuse me of throwing his suitcase out of the train."

"And did you?"

"Oh for heaven's sake! What do you think? What

would he have done had I gone in to grab his case? What would the other passengers have said?"

"So what did you tell him?"

"I told him to ring the police when we get to Wellington or Shrewsbury, and see how far he gets with his accusation. That shut him up."

"Yes, I imagine it would have. Sorry to have disturbed you."

In the guard's office, Hoyle said to Guard Hewson, "There's something else afoot, Gordon. Charlton has just accused Wolseley of throwing his suitcase out of the train, but Wolseley simply told him to report the matter to the police again."

Guard Hewson laughed. "Fat chance! The police could have him for harassment."

"Yes, that's what Wolseley told him. Hopefully, that will be the last of it all until Chester, then they can sort out matters themselves, without assistance from the Great Western Railway."

"Let's hope so, Mr Hoyle."

"Mind you, we should contact the Permanent Way people at Wellington to keep an eye out for a suitcase alongside the line, somewhere near Cosford, I should think."

"You don't think it was all a joke?"

"Actually, no, I don't. My son told me that he thought he saw a suitcase falling out of the train. He also thought he saw a gun yesterday, you might recall, and a gun was found later."

"Yes, that's right. Of course. I'll inform the

platform inspector; we should be arriving any minute now."

The train began to slow down and a couple of minutes later it pulled up at the main down platform at Wellington. Guard Hewson immediately stepped out of the train and went to the stationmaster's office, to report the possible loss of a suitcase somewhere near Cosford.

***

George and Lance were happier than they had expected to be. Their engine was performing well. They had been informed by Reg Bilsom that they would take their engine through to Chester without a change at Wolverhampton. It would return to Oxford on the Margate the following day.

"I've bin wonderin', Mr D," commented Lance as he shovelled more coal into the firebox, "wot's the right name fer our next stop? Is it Shroosbury or Shrowsbury? I've 'eard both."

Driver Denton paused and thought for a moment or two. "It depends on who you ask, Lance. If you listen to the BBC announcers, it's Shrowsbury, but if you talk to the people who live in the town, including my old grandfather, most will tell you it's Shroosbury. So that's what I always call the place."

"So real people call it Shroosbury, an' snobs call it Shrowsbury?"

George laughed, "You could say that."

"So wot are we, then, Mr D?"

"How do you mean?"

"Well, we can't be real people nor snobs can we, 'cos we railwaymen call the place Salop!"

"Ah, that was the old Roman name for the place."

"But the Romans was 'undreds of years back, and they didn't 'ave trains, did they?"

There was no answer to that, thought George Denton, so he didn't even try to compose one. "Let's see if we can pick up another minute or two."

Lance put another shovelful of coal into the firebox, muttering, "I 'ear an' obey!"

The lad was irrepressible, thought George as he glanced at the locomotive's speedometer and lifted the regulator slightly to increase the speed. Checking his watch, he noticed that they had cut almost five minutes off their delay, and they were now on the stretch of line which could allow greater speed.

"Only fifty minutes down now, Lance, and still the racing stretch between Salop and Baschurch to help, and then again between Wrexham and Chester. We might be able to cut off another ten or fifteen, if we're careful."

*****

In his compartment, Charlton was still fuming; he had to do something about that bastard who simply wouldn't leave him alone. He didn't know exactly how the man had taken his case. He had now not only lost his gun, but he was over a thousand quid down, not to mention that all his clothes were missing. These were not critical issues; he could easily replace all of this in Chester within a few days, but the man had irritated him beyond all reason, and was going to have to be dealt with once and for all. As his fellow passenger got up to take down his case from the luggage rack, an idea occurred to Charlton: he could perhaps make contact with Smith with a simple request. He would offer the neighbouring passenger a pound to make a phone call for him.

"Are you leaving the train in Shrewsbury?" he asked the man.

"Yes, that's right. I really am sorry I missed seeing who took your case."

"You could do me a small favour in return," Charlton suggested.

"I'd be happy to help, if I can."

"I need to urgently get in touch with someone on the phone, but the stop in Shrewsbury would be too short. Would you make the call for me?"

"Certainly. I'd be glad to."

"I'll cover your expense, of course. I'd like you to call a man in Chester and give him a short message. Would a pound be acceptable?"

The man was startled at the huge sum. "Very generous of you, but what if there's no reply?"

"Don't worry about that. You could leave a message, but I'm sure he will answer in person."

"Very well, I'll do it as soon as I get home. That would be in about half an hour."

"Er – could you do it from a call box at the station? It's fairly urgent."

"Alright, if it's that urgent."

"Thank you." Charlton reached into his wallet, took out a pound note, and handed it over. "I'll just scribble a short note for you to read to my friend. His name is Smith. Tell him Charlton asked you to call."

He wrote the phone number on the back of an envelope and underneath he wrote: 'Meet Wolseley, an elderly man in his seventies, off the Margate train. He is wearing a dark grey jacket and brown trousers and carries a haversack. He knows our business and needs to be rewarded for his efforts.'

Strange message, thought the passenger, *but it's none of my business*. To Charlton he just said, "I'll be sure to pass it on." He picked up his case as the train began to slow down on its approach to Shrewsbury. Leaving the compartment, he headed along the corridor to wait with a few other passengers by the door at the end of the coach. Once the train had stopped, he stepped out and headed for the stairs with the message securely in his hand. He knew there was a phone box on the platform, and would make the call from there.

***

As the train slowed down under the overall roof of the station, Jimmy gazed avidly out of the window, jumping up in excitement. "Look there, Dad! It's an LMS streamliner on that train!"

Mr Hoyle looked as well. "Ah yes, that train is for South Wales. The big streamliner will come off here, and the train will probably be taken further by a GWR Castle."

"I thought those big engines were blue or red," said Jimmy, disappointed.

"Well, they were before the war, Jimmy, but with the shortage of men, they painted them all black. I hope they will regain their old colours soon."

"I suppose that's why they're all dirty as well," said Jimmy glumly. Still, he could tell his friends that he had finally seen a big LMS streamliner; most of them hadn't.

His father was no longer listening, being more concerned with watching the passengers on the platform and hoping not to see either Wolseley or Charlton causing a stir. He noticed one man striding to the exit stairs with his case in one hand, and what looked like an envelope in the other, but apart from that, there was nothing else of note, for which he was very thankful.

Guard Gordon Hewson was equally relieved as he stood on the platform, also watching the passengers leaving and boarding his train, and deeming that there did not seem to be anything to concern him this time. There was no sign at all of either Wolseley or Charlton getting off the train, which meant that there was no reason to hold it any longer than necessary. He was pleased to see the starter signal showing clear at the far end of the platform. The signalmen were doing their best to help them. As soon as the last passenger had boarded, he blew his whistle and waved his green flag. The train began to move instantly, he noticed; George and Lance were obviously eager to try and make up lost time and he knew they were in for a fast run; he had travelled behind the team of Denton and Hargreaves before and was well aware of what they were capable.

CHAPTER 10

A Final Resolution

As the train pulled away from Shrewsbury, Wolseley felt an increasing pressure on his bladder. "Must pop off to the WC," he muttered to himself, and left the compartment. In the toilet, he realised he had left his haversack in the compartment and there was no-one else there. Charlton could easily nip in and pinch it, but what good would that do him? There was nothing in the haversack that would be of any conceivable use to the man, except possibly some pills. Wolseley shook his head. In any case, there was no use worrying now; the haversack would be gone, or it would not. It wasn't a serious problem; he had Charlton's money in his jacket pocket. He rinsed his hands, returned to his seat, checked the rack and found that yes, his haversack had gone. "The bugger's nicked it," he said loudly. This was a nuisance, but nothing more; the clothes wouldn't even fit Charlton, and the pills – well, he could do what he liked with them. One of those wouldn't do him any harm. In this matter, however, Wolseley was seriously in error.

One of the previous passengers had left a newspaper on the seat, so Wolseley picked it up and began to read. He had decided to take no further action himself; he knew where Charlton lived, and he had sufficient information on both Charlton and Smith to pass on to the police, which would enable them to find the evidence they needed to charge both with murder.

***

At about the same time Wolseley was returning to his seat, the phone rang in an unremarkable detached house in Chester.

Walter Smith lifted the receiver. "Yes?"

"Am I speaking to a Mr Smith?"

"Yes, that's me. Who is talking?"

"You don't know me, but I have been asked by a gentleman on the train at Shrewsbury, which I have just left, to pass on an urgent message to you."

"I see. What is the message?"

"The man's name is Charlton and the message reads... now, just a moment, let me get it from my pocket... ah, here it is –" he read the scrawled note verbatim – "I hope that means something to you."

"Yes, I understand. Thank you."

"A highly profitable day!" Charlton's messenger had paid less than two bob for the call, and he looked at the pound note in pleasure. He was eighteen shillings richer as he scrunched up the envelope and dropped it into a rubbish bin on his way.

"Sometimes," he muttered to himself with a grin, "you just get lucky!"

Smith hadn't recognised the voice on the line, and had been immediately on his guard. However, when he heard the message and Charlton's name, Smith understood that Charlton had got himself into a difficult situation. He didn't care about that, and wouldn't normally have bothered to assist, but what was far more to the point was that this character Wolseley knew about their activities. He would have to be dealt with – and quickly.

Smith took his car from the garage and drove to Chester General Station, to check the time of the arrival of the Margate train on Platform Three. It was due in just before six o'clock, in time to get himself a cup of tea in the refreshment room and wait for the train's arrival. He patted his inside pocket to check that his pistol was there, and that the safety catch was on. He didn't want any accidental shots fired.

There were only two possible exits from the platform. One was up and over the footbridge to the Hoole exit, although not many people would use that one, and the other was along the platform to the main exit. He positioned himself there. He had memorised the details of Wolseley's appearance, and had no fear that he would miss the man, but even if he did, he could always get the bloke's address from his mate in the police.

***

Jimmy Hoyle, watching out of the window, yawned as his father smiled at him. The lad had been busy all day, and the excitement of the last thirty hours was beginning to take its toll. May had been sound asleep for over an hour already. They would be home before 7:00 pm, and the children would go straight to bed without complaint.

Thankfully, it was also beginning to look as if there would be no more disturbances from those two difficult passengers. But Mr Hoyle's conclusion, like that of Wolseley, was to prove incorrect.

***

Charlton had prowled up and down the corridor once or twice, and had noticed Wolseley going to the toilet. He had used the opportunity to grab Wolseley's haversack and take it into the toilet in his own coach, where he examined the contents. He was hoping to recover his money and was very disappointed not to find it. All he could see were useless clothing items and some pills whose packet indicated that they were for relaxation. "Might be able to use those," he muttered, putting the packet into his pocket, "but there's nothing else here!"

He took the haversack into the corridor, opened a window, and hurled it out, smiling for the first time in hours and quoting, "Sauce for the goose is sauce for the gander!" Gleefully, he went back to his seat and relaxed, waiting for an angry Wolseley to show up. For once, he was going to enjoy meeting the blighter.

By this time, the train was speeding past Whittington. Charlton was looking out of the window, pondering over the last couple of days and hoping that Smith would be ready at Chester to rid them both of the annoying Wolseley. He wondered again why on earth the man had been pursuing him so doggedly. Had that black-market medication killed a relative, perhaps? His persistence had been frankly very alarming.

Considering the level of stress he had been under for the past forty-eight hours, Charlton wondered whether he should take a couple of those pills he had found in Wolseley's haversack. *Why not?* He badly needed to relax. Going to the toilet once more for a drink of water, he popped not one but five of Wolseley's pills into his mouth. Then he returned to his seat and settled down to doze off and let the pills work their magic.

***

Driver George Denton checked his watch again as the train drew in at Ruabon Station. He smiled and glanced over to his fireman. "We've picked up another seven minutes, Lance. If you can keep your end up, we might be able to cut our delay into Chester to only forty."

Lance grinned back. "Yer can rely on me, Mr D." He shook his shoulders to relax them then checked the steam pressure, nodding to himself; there was still plenty of steam for the engine to bite on. He added another five shovelfuls of coal around the firebox while they were standing still, to be ready for the demands of the locomotive when they got the 'right away'.

George watched as Lance worked, thinking again what an excellent driver he would make one day. It was time to start thinking about improving the lad's vocabulary and demeanour.

"We'll 'ave the day off termorrer 'an I've got a new bird ter take out. Me thoughts are on 'ow I can get 'er ter see things my way."

George shook his head. A perfect illustration of his areas of concern. "I don't think you'll ever learn, Lance. I recall you had your eye on a girl on a Salop train once and you tried to chat her up, then her powerful bloke wanted to dissuade you with his fist!"

Lance blinked. "Oh aye, I remember you saved me bacon that day. You told 'im I was on the Birken'ead run, when I was 'idin' be'ind the engine!"

"Yes, I believe I did."

The guard's whistle sounded, and they eased their train away and picked up speed rapidly.

"We can gain a minute or two before Wrexham if we're lucky, but the final run down Gresford Bank will give us a chance to pick up a few more minutes."

While he was explaining this, Lance had the pricker out, and was raking the fire to move the coal to where it would give the most heat. George nodded his approval.

***

While they were standing at the platform in Ruabon, Wolseley had been carefully studying the passengers on the platform, to see whether Charlton was doing anything suspicious. He didn't see anything to raise his suspicions and, after waiting till the train moved off again, just to be certain, he sat down, pondering.

There was something at the back of his mind, and he tried to concentrate on what it was. He had been a detective long enough to know that his brain sometimes registered important details without him being aware of them at the time. Suddenly, he had it: he recalled seeing a passenger leaving the train at Shrewsbury, and hurrying along the platform. The man had a slip of paper in his hand. Why was that significant? Why had his brain picked that up? Where had he seen the man before, anyway?

Of course! It was the sleeping passenger from Charlton's compartment when Wolseley had nicked the case. Was it possible that the man might have been persuaded by Charlton to make a phone call on his behalf? Wolseley would put a pound to a penny that the phone call would be to Walter Smith, who Charlton said had supplied the lethal component of the black-market drugs. He would further bet that Smith might well be waiting for him at Chester Station. Well, Mr Smith was going to be disappointed; Wolseley would certainly be getting out in Chester, but not at the General Station. He would disembark at Northgate!

The next stop was Wrexham General, and

Wolseley cautiously left the train, looking back to Charlton's coach and hoping the man wouldn't notice him. In any event, it wouldn't matter too much, because he wouldn't be able warn Smith in time. Wolseley needn't have worried: Charlton was dead to the world.

***

Gordon Hewson noticed this with pleasure as he checked the tickets of passengers who had boarded the train in Wrexham. He had already been pleased to see Wolseley disembarking at Wrexham. "No further problems from those men," he said softly to himself as he walked along the corridor. But such an optimistic prediction, like those others had made before him, was to prove inaccurate.

***

At Wrexham Exchange Station, Wolseley crossed over to the LNER platforms and boarded a connecting train which, an hour later, arrived at Chester Northgate, where he took a taxi to Police Headquarters to see his successor. Valuable information was quickly passed over.

***

Lance was enjoying himself in the cab. His driver was known to be one of the best in the whole division, and this was obvious from the way he was coaxing the locomotive to do its best. They were racing down the bank, past the little station at Rossett, and were soon across the Dee plain, ready for the slight uphill run through Saltney. They had to slow for the curve to join the main LMS line to North Wales at Saltney Junction but were able to put on a little more speed through the long cutting and over the Dee Bridge.

He looked with a smirk at his driver. "We'll be in Deva in four minutes, Mr D."

"Deva?"

"Roman name fer Chester; din'tcher know?"

George Denton shut his eyes in sheer delight. For the hundredth time, he breathed a sigh of pleasure that he was partnered with Lance Hargreaves. Not only was his fireman extremely competent; the lad was a constant source of entertainment.

***

Gordon Hewson decided to ensure that his troublesome passenger definitely left the train at his Chester destination, and as they pulled into Chester General, he walked along to Charlton's compartment. But the man showed no sign of getting up. He was fast asleep.

"Mr Charlton, sir. We've arrived in Chester. Your ticket does not permit you to travel further."

Charlton slept on.

"Wake up, sir. We're in Chester."

Guard Hewson tapped the man's shoulder gently.

Charlton slowly rolled over, and slipped to the floor.

"God almighty, the man's dead!" Hewson grunted and went to find Hoyle, who was ushering his sleepy children onto the platform. This wasn't the first deceased passenger he had seen on his trains.

"It's Charlton!" hissed the guard urgently, trying to make sure the children didn't hear. "He's dead!"

"Bugger!" exclaimed Hoyle and his son started at his language. "Jimmy, go with May to the ticket collector at the gate, tell him there's been an emergency on the train, and to look after you two while Mr Hewson and I sort this out. Quickly, now!"

Jimmy wordlessly grabbed his sister's hand, and they hurried to the exit.

***

Smith, waiting on Platform Three, saw nobody fitting the description he had been given. He was not, however, overly concerned. *I can get the address of that bloke Wolseley from my bent copper mate,* he decided, *then I can pay the man a visit and shut him up permanently.*

Then he saw the guard and another man, who seemed to be some sort of official, with police and ambulancemen carrying somebody – who looked decidedly similar in shape and size to Charlton – out of the train.

Stupid bugger's too fat anyway, he thought to himself, but he didn't like the look of things, and hurried back to his car. He noted the ambulance outside the station and drove straight home. There, he was concerned to see a police car outside his house, with a policeman standing by.

It was too late to drive past; the policeman had clearly seen him. "This your house, sir?"

"Yes. What of it?"

"I'd like you to come with me, sir. My inspector would like to ask you a few questions."

Smith slipped his hand into his pocket and felt his gun. A quick shot and he could be away before more police could be summoned. He quietly eased the safety switch off but as he swiftly pulled the gun from his pocket to fire, he was distracted by a call from his house.

"In here, Jack! We've got the evidence we need!"

Smith's bullet missed its target, hitting the policeman's shoulder.

The wounded police constable gasped as he fell. Hearing the shot, two of his colleagues hurried out of the house and, while one ran for Smith's car, the other hurled himself at Smith, whose second shot went straight into the air as he was tackled to the ground. The policeman recovered quickly and stamped on Smith's gun-hand, forcing him to drop the weapon. Smith was soon handcuffed and pushed into the police car.

Walter Smith was an intelligent man of some imagination, and he knew perfectly well that, after a few weeks in a prison cell, he would spend three or four days in court. There would be no doubt at all about the verdict. Perhaps a week after that, he would undertake a short walk through the prison, accompanied by warders, a prison official, and a priest, to a closed room.

This room would contain a trapdoor with a noose hanging above it, and for him there would be no return.

***

Two days after his return, Wolseley's phone rang. "Yes?"

"Henderson here, Roger. I have a dead man on a train from the South; oddly enough, a train I believe you were on. I've also two injured uniforms, and a bloke in the cells we've been after for months. What do you know about all this?"

"Me, sir? I'm retired. What would I know about a police matter?"

D.S. Henderson laughed. "I've known you since you were a sergeant on the beat, Roger. This has your name all over it."

"Perhaps you should ask my successor. I've told him all I know."

"No you haven't, you lying sod. Danny's not a bad copper, but he hasn't got your nose. I've booked a table for two at the Grosvenor tomorrow at seven; you can tell me everything then, off the record."

"I'll be there, sir."

Over a delicious meal, Wolseley told Superintendent Henderson the story of his trip to Margate. The latter nodded. "You did very well, Roger, but you were lucky. I don't think you would have been in serious danger from Charlton, but Smith is a different matter. He is vicious, and tried to kill two officers. Your clever changing of trains at Wrexham foiled him."

"I was fortunate spotting that passenger with the message at Shrewsbury, sir. That's all."

"That's as may be. By the way, what have you done with all that money you pinched off Charlton? About a thousand, wasn't it?"

"Money, sir? I don't recall mentioning any money."

Henderson laughed. "No, you didn't. But I noticed an unusually large anonymous donation to the Police Widows and Families Association, yesterday. A thousand pounds, if my memory serves me correctly."

"I have no comment to make on that, sir."

"Very wise, Roger, very wise."

Also by Michael Clutterbuck

The Steaming Into Series:
a fantastic collection of tales from the rails

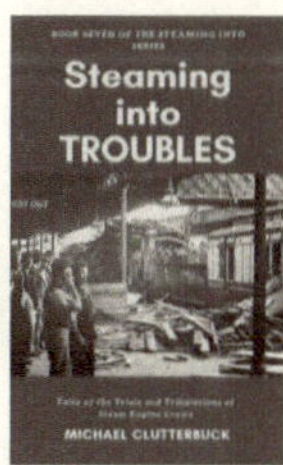